Temple Bells

Other Books by Marjorie McEvoy

STAR OF RANDEVI
THE SLEEPING TIGER
CALABRIAN SUMMER
ECHOES FROM THE PAST

Temple Bells

MARJORIE MCEVOY

DOUBLEDAY & COMPANY, INC.
GARDEN CITY, NEW YORK
1985

Library of Congress Cataloging in Publication Data

McEvoy, Marjorie.
Temple bells.

I. Title.
PR6063.A196T4   1985   823'.914
ISBN 0-385-23027-3
Library of Congress Catalog Card Number 85-6816

This is for Joe

Temple Bells

CHAPTER ONE

Chantra. 1766

High up on the soaring, golden spire of the *chedi,* the tiny wind bells shivered in the warm breath of the breeze that floated up the Chao Phraya River from the Gulf of Thailand. The music was enchanting.

The breeze did nothing to cool the sultry heat. It must be ninety-five degrees at least, Chantra reflected, feeling the perspiration trickling down her back. High time they went home to the midday meal at the Chandra Kasem Palace, standing just outside the walls of Ayutthaya on the northeast corner of the city.

Today, on this shining September morning in the year 1766, was her seventeenth birthday. She was growing up, and already experiencing the half-understood secret longings that came with budding maturity. For the first time she felt a wave of irritation at the narrowness of this life of hers, spent with six young cousins in the charge of a governess. No longer did it bring any thrill to saunter round the chedis and monasteries, or sail down the *klongs* to the floating market in their company. The city, capital of all Siam, was a dream with its graceful spires of gold and marble, and bright mosaics, its smiling people with their great straw hats, its saffron-robed monks walking in file, their begging bowls held ready in their hands. It had been enough until now. Her whole world.

Now she felt a distinct yearning to go off on her own and explore the country beyond: The many klongs lined with little wooden houses built high on stilts where humble folk lived like ants in an ant heap. The lush jungles garlanded with wild orchids and great gaudy butterflies. The foreign trading posts near the city, where British, Dutch, French and Chinese ships lay at anchor, having sailed halfway around the world and up the broad Chao Phraya river to sell their machinery and other sophisticated wares, and return with cargoes of teak, rice and cotton.

Oh, most of all did she long to see these trading stations, for the ships were captained by strange, tall, pale-skinned Westerners who put the Siamese men to shame, making them seem like coffee-colored pigmies. Like the British Ambassador who had once come to dine at the palace of her uncle, Crown Prince Jayavarman, and of whom she had caught a fleeting glimpse.

Chantra took a keen interest in Britain, for not only had she learned a passable amount of English from her half-British governess, but also a fascinating smattering of the history of that strange country across the oceans, where the winter winds froze the water solid and a white substance called snow covered the land like a blanket.

The Siamese were an advanced and friendly people, she realized with pride. They welcomed foreigners and the trade that brought wealth to their country. Not for the first time she wished with all her heart that she had been born a boy, so that she, too, could become a sailor explorer, or go off to fight the Burmese, who constantly threatened their peaceful existence with unexpected raids.

"Do stop dawdling and keep up with the rest of us, Chantra," Miss Bradbury, the governess, called sharply. "We are off to see the White Elephant now. You shall all give him a banana and then we'll return to the palace. I confess I shall be glad to retire to some shade."

She had purchased a bunch of bananas from a fruit vendor outside the Wat Phra Chao Phanan for the express purpose of giving them this treat. The White Elephant was revered and pampered by all, but the sight of it had lost its magic for Chantra. Yet she trailed obediently after her cousins, past the Suriyat Amarinda, shining in its gilded splendor, to the stable of the great beast who lived like a king.

Here, they each in turn presented a banana, which the gentle giant accepted with its trunk, transferred the tidbit to its mouth and gave a resounding trumpet of thanks for each offering.

Chantra smiled in spite of herself, an elfin smile that transformed her piquant little face into enchanting beauty beneath its mop of black curls. How outraged Miss Bradbury had been when the girl had slashed off her long plaits one day in defiance of so much brushing and fussing at bedtime. But how deliciously cool Chantra had felt without them. It had been well worth the punishment of a hundred lines.

Now they were back at the small Chandra Kasem Palace, where all the Crown Princes had lived since 1577. This would never have been her home had her own parents been alive, Miss Bradbury was all too fond of reminding her. Since typhoid had carried them off ten years ago, she had enjoyed the privileges of palace life, in spite of being often reminded that she was only here on sufferance, the poor relation, not quite one of the family.

They entered the palace through a side door guarded by fearsome stone monsters, and made their way to a secluded suite of rooms at the rear. One half housed the harem of Crown Prince Jayavarman, the other was given over to the royal children and their governess. These rooms opened into a walled courtyard, shaded by flowering frangipani trees and centered by a small pool covered with pink and white lotus blooms. A delectable spot where the children played in safety and the ladies of the harem could lounge unseen by any male eyes.

Now, in the heat of midday, it was deserted. The dim shuttered rooms held more appeal.

A meal of rice, various spicy dishes and sliced pineapple was served at the low table. After it the children were whisked away by Miss Bradbury to their shaded dormitory to rest for the afternoon.

"I advise you to do the same," she cautioned Chantra. "I shall be quite relieved when you are married and off my hands. It is a great pity there is no one to arrange it for you, but it will have to be done sooner or later."

Chantra made a wry face as the governess vanished with her brood. She had no intention of retiring to the small austere room that was all she could call her own in this sumptuous place. Of late she had taken to stealing out alone while the palace was quiet under the influence of the afternoon siesta. There was a shady arbor in the grounds where she could lie in the long cane chair and dream to her heart's content, without fear of interruption, for even the gardeners took a brief nap under the spreading banyan tree.

Today this was not enough. She felt like a bird that must stretch its wings and fly off to explore the world alone. Outside the palace were the klongs, flowing serenely to many attractions. It would be cool and delightful paddling alone along one of these, and that was what she would do.

Miss Bradbury never ventured farther than the floating market, where almost anything could be bought from the flat-bottomed boats crowding together. Interesting enough, but today was a landmark, Chantra reflected. Seventeen years old, and almost a woman, she must do something different to mark the occasion.

A daring thought grew to tantalize her. In the opposite direction, the broad, deep Chao Phraya flowed downstream to the sea, passing the various foreign trading stations on the way. A trip that way should be rewarding, showing seagoing vessels anchored at their bases. With luck, even a glimpse of some of those tall bearded sailors might be caught.

Excitement gripped her, but of course she must have some disguise. Since she was not a seller of fruit or any other commodity, a girl alone might attract unwelcome attention. What should she wear?

A glance in the cupboard revealed Miss Bradbury's capacious mending basket, with several garments waiting for attention. There was even a pair of baggy blue breeches belonging to Prince Sithi, the eldest of the royal princes, together with a loose white shirt. They both had small rents, sustained while he played among bushes in the palace grounds.

Though several years younger than she, the prince was tall for his age. Chantra knew that her own petite figure would fit easily into the garments and, with the flat-topped straw hat she wore in the garden, would perfectly disguise her as a boy.

With fast-beating heart, she tore off the *pasin,* a strip of vivid batik that encircled her waist and fell to her ankles like a sarong, and stepped into the blue breeches. Of the usual Siamese design, they were mid-calf length, and baggy enough around the seat to allow the wearer to squat down cross-legged in comfort in the lotus position of the Buddha.

How strange it felt to be free of the impeding long skirt. Laughing, she capered around in her embroidered slippers, then pulled off her blouse and donned instead the loose jacket that buttoned up the front to the mandarin collar. The addition of the big straw hat completed her disguise. She was the perfect boy to all save the closest examination.

The small store of accumulated pocket money in her room now promised to unlock the door to escape. She could hire a boat or anything else that took her fancy. She stuffed some of the *ticals* into the breeches pocket and stole out into the deserted courtyard.

Once free of the palace grounds, she made a beeline for the small boat station on the klong. Here one could hire a boat, complete with paddler, for a reasonable sum. For a much smaller amount, a boat could be hired and the hirer steer himself wherever he wished to go with the long unwieldy-looking pole.

Chantra paid her ticals and climbed into one of these, wanting to be on her own. The paddle proved awkward and difficult at first, and she hugged the klong edge, close to the wooden shacks whose steps led straight down into the water.

On the wooden platforms above, the peasants cooked, ate or slept, protected from the sun by rice straw thatches and the coconut and banana palms that pressed closely about them, their great green leaves hanging over the water. Naked children, scorning a siesta, sported at the edge of the murky water. Living as much in it as out, they could all swim like fishes.

No one took the slightest notice of the apparent boy poling awkwardly along. As soon as she began to get the hang of it, Chantra moved out into mid-stream, steering herself in and out of the other craft, and made for the Chao Phraya River.

Once on its broad bosom, she felt less restricted. Although it teemed with vessels of all kinds, there was still plenty of room to maneuver and choose a clear lane. Exhilaration filled her. For the first time she felt free and unrestricted. Master of herself and her wishes.

Soon the trading stations came in sight. Interest quickened, she moved closer to the bank, staring avidly at the sailing vessels with their tall masts moored alongside.

It was awe-inspiring to realize that these graceful, frail-looking craft could sail halfway around the world, manned by the exciting strange beings of whom she caught glimpses, scrubbing down decks, mending sails or even climbing the soaring masts as agilely as the monkeys that shinned up the coconut palms here in Siam. Clad only in bell-bottomed trousers, their broad, hairy chests burned brown by the sun, they sang a lively sea shanty as they worked that sounded odd in this tropical setting.

This was the British trading post. She knew by the Union Jack fluttering from the teak sheds on the bank. She paused in her paddling to gaze her fill, wishing that she knew more about the great world beyond the Gulf of Siam.

And then, from out of the nearest shed stepped a man who brought a gasp of admiration from the watching girl. Clad in tropical white, with immaculate duck slacks, gold-braid-trimmed jacket and smart peaked cap, he stood out, a king among his minions.

Unlike most of them, he wore no beard. His handsome face was tanned just sufficiently by the sun to add to his attraction. Never, reflected Chantra, had she seen such a man before. He was surely the captain of the ship, his word law until he returned to his home port, his orders to be obeyed promptly without question.

Seeing her staring up from the small boat, he stopped his jaunty whistling and descended the steps to the brief wooden jetty.

"Hey, boy, are you for hire?" he asked in English, and then: "Damnation! He won't understand a word I say."

"Indeed I do, sir," Chantra assured him.

He laughed, showing white teeth. "Incredible! I know this is a go-ahead nation, but one doesn't expect the coolies to be so advanced as to speak foreign languages!"

"Most of them are not. I just happen to have an English

friend," she explained, unwilling to give away the fact that she lived in a palace, was a girl and had a half-English governess.

"Lucky for me! Tell me, do you know the ruins of Mongkor?"

"Of course. What Siamese does not!"

"Are they close enough to get there and back before dark?"

She nodded.

"I've heard that the main chedi is the tallest in all Siam. I'd like to boast when I get back home that I'd seen it. If you'll take me there and back, you can name your own price."

Excitement gripped her. It would be a pleasure to take him for nothing. Here was adventure with a vengeance. The very stuff that dreams are made of.

"Step in," she said, moving close to the jetty and striving to keep the elation from her voice. "We shan't haggle over money."

He stepped down and took the second seat in the prow of the narrow boat. Like all the other boat steerers on the klong, Chantra occupied the rear seat, plying her long pole from there. She was glad of this arrangement, as it meant that he was looking ahead and so had his back to her. She would have felt distinctly nervous about his penetrating her disguise had be been seated facing her in such close proximity.

He took off his smart cap and mopped his brow, asking, "When does it get cooler here, if it ever does?"

She smiled. "Now the monsoon is over, it will be a little cooler soon. The change from England must be awful. Is this your first voyage to Siam?"

"It is. My first commission and ship, actually. I was highly elated to join the East India Company. It means sailing to such exciting places."

"Will you be staying here long?" She hoped the answer would be yes.

"Oh, a week or so to unload and pick up cargo, then a call at Madras on the way back for spices and silks. Now stop chattering and let me concentrate on the sights. I've never seen such an interesting river."

The Chao Phraya was certainly that. Great, deeply laden rice barges, with their low-domed tops, sailed sluggishly along in convoy. Small boats such as the one they occupied, piled high with produce and steered by a single occupant, maneuvered in and out, pausing now and then to make sales to the dwellers in the little wooden shacks lining the banks. Women washed clothes, pots and themselves. Men fished and poled their narrow little boats through the malodorous river that was their main means of communication.

He wrinkled his nose at the latter. "This water must be swarming with germs! No wonder so many of the East India Company personnel have short lives, coming out to these countries. Say, boy, do you live in one of those shacks?"

"Of course not!" Just in time she stopped herself from adding, "I live in the small palace, second only to the king's," and substituted, "I live on the edge of the city of Ayutthaya. It is the capital and the greatest city in Siam."

"So I gather. I'm more interested in the surrounding country and the ancient ruins than in cities, however. And now that I've discovered you, a real find with your knowledge of English, I should see quite a bit of it before sailing again. My duties are light while at anchor, so I hope you're available most days."

"Most afternoons," Chantra agreed. Disguised in boyish garb, she should be able to slip away while Miss Bradbury and her charges were indulging in their siesta, without difficulty.

"Splendid." He broke off to stare at a colorful *wat* they were passing, with its graceful spires and fantastic eaves. Monks in saffron robes could be seen going about their business.

"They belong to the monastery attached to the wat," Chantra explained. "Most Siamese men, even the kings, spend a short time of their lives as monks. It is supposed to teach them humility, among other things."

The river grew less congested. The waterside shacks petered out, and then the scene became wholly rural, with thick jungle on either side pressing right down to the river's edge. The few rice barges and other craft kept out in mid-stream, sailing steadily on their way to the sea.

Presently, Chantra propelled them to the bank, where a rough landing place had been formed from bamboo poles protruding over the water. They scrambled ashore. She tied up the boat and led the way through a tangle of coconut palms, flowering shrubs, festooning vines and exotic orchids.

"This is the ruin of Mongkor Wat," she explained. "I don't know how long they've been decaying or who was responsible. For centuries neighboring countries have made sporadic raids on Siam. They envy us our prosperity. Just now it is the Burmese who are threatening us, but I don't think they'll ever succeed in conquering us."

Captain James Stuart was not so certain. The Burmese were a desperate nation, hemmed in by powerful neighbors like China and India. Annexation of a country like Siam would add appreciable strength in every way.

But politics were forgotten when they emerged from the jungle strip on to a wide arena of rough ground. Here, in various stages of decay, stood chedis, temples and buildings of various sizes, the graceful remaining spires that had stood the test of time rising triumphantly to the sky.

An air of nostalgic desolation lay over all. Nature's healing hand had taken over, softening the broken walls and fallen masonry with jungle flowers, and grasses, wild myrtles and the waxy blooms of frangipani. Strange, harsh-voiced birds called from the jasmines, while green and gray lizards sunned themselves on the hot stones.

And over all towered the great chedi, defying time and the elements, and the serene, broken Buddhas.

The captain stood in awe. "It's like a petrified dream," he murmured at last.

She nodded. "I love these ruins, too. All gray stone and silence. So different to the gaudy buildings of Ayutthaya, with their bustle and pomp. I could wander around every day, just dreaming of the past."

"I understand." After the austere life at sea, battling with the elements, cramped in a confined space with no other company than rough sailors, this was another world. A world of mysticism, peace and events lost in the mists of time.

"Old, forgotten, far-off things,
And battles long ago,"

he murmured, wondering where he had heard it before. It could have been describing this very spot.

They began to saunter around, speaking little, simply absorbing the wonder, the beauty, the utter silence, the outside world left behind.

Presently, some creeper-grown broken steps at the base of a half-ruined chedi tempted them to climb. They ascended as far as they could go in safety, and stood drinking in the view of the ruins stretching around them on every side.

"Now I shall have plenty to boast about when I at last reach home," he said, turning to descend.

Home. She was distastefully reminded of siesta time back at the palace, and that it was swiftly passing. Time to be getting back if she were not to be caught sneaking in attired in a pair of her cousin's breeches.

The thought made her press ahead and hurry down without due caution. The last step was some way off the ground. She leaped it carelessly and would have stumbled and fallen had not James Stuart, close behind, reached out instinctively and grabbed her around the middle.

Suddenly, he became very still, his hands unexpectedly encountering two small, budding breasts instead of a firm boyish chest. The soft warmth of them beneath the thin shirt took his breath away.

When he regained it, he spun her around, still encircled in his arms.

"You're no boy," he murmured. "They're just not made like that."

Fear, shame and discomfort all showed in the crestfallen little face.

"Don't be angry," she said at last. "I had to disguise myself to escape for a brief while. I felt so stifled and cut off."

"Angry!" He laughed softly. "Why, it's quite marvelous! You can't imagine how one longs for a little sweet feminine company on those interminable sea voyages. I count myself fortunate indeed. That is, if you won't let it make any difference to our arrangement. You'll still take me around while I'm here, won't you?"

She looked doubtful.

"Oh come! You can still wear the breeches, and only I will know the truth!"

Suddenly she laughed too. "How can I say no? I've never been friends with a man before. It's terribly exciting!"

"You're very sweet, and young." He threw off her big straw hat and ruffled her rioting black curls.

"Now you look quite enchanting. Tell me your name. Your real name."

"Chantra," she whispered.

"As enchanting as you." The words were muffled, for his mouth was against hers, pressing, pressing until her warm lips parted and he seemed to be drawing the very breath from her body.

She felt languorous and weak. Only his arms around her upheld her. Only his face—tanned, firm—filled her entire world. This firm, ecstatic kiss burst upon her like the first flash of lightning in a monsoon thunderstorm. Unexpected, wonderful, shattering.

"We should be getting back," she said at last in a strange little voice that did not sound like her own, "or I'll be in hot water."

He began to walk on, his arm around her still.

"Tell me about your home," he insisted. "You're no coolie, any more than you're a boy. Cultured, educated, enchanting enough to be a princess herself."

She smiled. "Actually, you are quite near the mark. I'm the poor cousin of princes and princesses at least, and live in the palace of the Crown Prince. I slipped out in disguise this afternoon while they and their governess are sleeping, just for a birthday treat, really."

"This is your birthday?"

"Really and truly. I'm seventeen."

"This grows more and more like a fairy tale. I must get you a present before I have to leave."

"It will have to be something small that I can hide, then," she said gravely. "Miss Bradbury would be outraged if she so much as suspected I was leaving the palace grounds on my own, let alone wandering around with a man. She's the half-English governess."

"She sounds as formidable as those in England."

"Normally I should be married by now, to someone chosen by my parents, but as I'm an orphan, and the Crown Prince's wife is dead too, no one has troubled to arrange it."

"Thank heaven for that. You're too young and pretty to be tied down to someone who would crush all the spirit out of you. Much more fun to marry for love, I'd say."

She shook her head. "This is Siam. Love does not come into it. Only rank, and dowries. I have no dowry, so perhaps I shall be an old maid before long."

He laughed. "I'd say the odds were a hundred to one against."

They reached the boat and embarked on the river. She punted him to his trading post and dropped him, promising to come again the following afternoon if she could get away unseen.

Fate was with her. She reached the palace, sped through the grounds and into her room without meeting a soul and just managed to divest herself of the breeches and put on her pasin, or skirt, before one of her young cousins burst in to demand that she join them in the courtyard for a ball game.

The following afternoon she repeated the subterfuge, as soon as Miss Bradbury and her brood had retired. She hurried out, again hired a small boat and found James Stuart waiting for her on the landing stage.

Her heartbeat quickened at the sight of his thrilling figure. Already, after only one meeting, his face haunted her like some strange secret rapture. Had he not been there, desolation would have claimed her for the rest of the day.

After a brief discussion, he expressed a wish to see the water market on the other side of the city. Had he asked for the moon, she would have tried to satisfy him. The water market was simple enough and could easily be fit into the short time at her disposal, so she began to pole the boat in that direction.

Care was needed in passing the city, where the river was congested with cumbersome rice barges, sampans, junks and smaller craft. The slow progress was no hardship, leaving time to take in the wonderful profile passing by, dominated by the graceful spires and towers of wats and chedis, palaces and monasteries.

Presently these were left behind, and only smaller craft poled their graceful way up or down the river, making their way to or from the market with produce and commodities of all kinds.

The market itself, when reached, was an animated scene, full of interest to James. Even Chantra, used as she was to the sight, never failed to find pleasure in the many little boats crowding the banks, each with its single punter in great straw hat, the rest of the space given over to piles of fruit or vegetables, gaily painted paper parasols, straw baskets and hats, embroidered sandals or lengths of brightly stamped batik.

Buyers thronged the banks, haggling over prices and driving hard bargains with the vendors. Coolies from the tiny dwellings crowding the opposite bank floated over in their own boats seeking various commodities to sustain their simple lives.

"Why, there's even a cookboat!" James laughed, pointing out the vessel.

It was flat-bottomed like the rest, holding several brass pots standing on charcoal burners, from which came savory smells. Meat, fruit and vegetables were stacked around, the raw ingredients of the owner's trade.

Chantra nodded. "Oh yes. She sells hot tea, curry, rice, cooked lentils and other things. They're quite good, too."

They poled around for a while, James greatly diverted by the strange sights, then tied up their boat and strolled around the village shacks backing the river in the shade of the encroaching jungle.

Chickens, pigs and dogs shared the one-room hovels with the owners, grunting and clucking around in the eternal quest for food, while grubby, naked children played among the rotting vegetation and odorous puddles.

"It's much nicer on the river," he said, wrinkling his nose at the stagnant smell and leading the way back to their boat.

A passing vendor of flowers smiled on seeing his smart uniform and Western face and held up a wreath of jasmine. It was quite beautiful, with a delightful perfume, and quite irresistible.

James took the wreath and passed over some coins.

"You should have bargained," Chantra admonished. "You'd have got it for half that."

"No matter, as it is to adorn the person of the prettiest girl in Siam." Laughing, he placed it round her neck, adding, "Now I'll always remember you looking so angelic that I'm longing to kiss you."

"We're in a public place, remember, and I'm supposed to be a boy." She picked up the pole and began to ease them dexterously out of the mass of river traffic, adding, "But as both sexes wear them on important or holiday occasions, no one will take any notice of the flowers."

"Can't we find a more private place and laze and chat?"

She shook her head. "I only have a limited time, you know. Just time to get past the city, deposit you at your station and return before the women's quarters of the palace is astir again. If they once suspect my deception, I'll be a prisoner from then on."

He sighed. "Well, there's always tomorrow. You promise to come?"

"If I possibly can."

All too soon they reached the wooden landing stage of his station.

"*Sawadee,*" she murmured as he climbed out.

"Which means?"

"Goodbye, or good morning, or hello."

"I'll remember that. Perhaps you can teach me a few more words before I have to leave this magical land."

"Perhaps." She felt as deflated as he at having to part without a touch of hands or lips, but a couple of sailors were working on his ship, covertly watching, so she was forced to pole herself away, with only a wave as his motionless figure receded.

This time she was not so lucky at gaining her room undetected. Miss Bradbury was emerging into the courtyard just as she hurried across it.

The governess stared in surprise.

"What on earth are you doing dressed in such a fashion and where have you been?" she demanded sternly.

Chantra thought fast, then said as innocently as she could manage, "Why, just around the grounds. I wanted to explore among the bushes in the wilder part and skirts are so restricting. I thought breeches would be easier to get about in."

"You are too bold for your own good, and behave more like seven than seventeen," the other scolded. "Never do anything so unbecoming again. I do wish your uncle would arrange a marriage for you. I have quite enough to do with the younger ones. Now go to your room and make yourself presentable before anyone else sees you or we shall both be in trouble."

Chantra went, glad that she had reluctantly left the beautiful flower wreath in the boat. It would have been difficult explaining that away.

The following morning at breakfast Miss Bradbury dashed all hope of any escape that day by remarking, "We are all to have a rare treat today. The Crown Prince has important visitors, and is entertaining them as usual with a display by his fighting elephants. He is graciously reserving seats for us to watch the show. In view of this, our siesta will be short today, to give us all time to dress carefully in our best. The entertainment will begin at five o'clock. You must be ready by half past four, so that we can reach the elephant arena and be in our places before the entrance of the prince and his guests."

The children clapped their hands, but Chantra was plunged into gloom. Not only did she hate elephant fighting, considering it cruel, but it meant there would be no chance of her slipping out and meeting her thrilling captain today. It was galling to picture him waiting there, first in hope then in growing disappointment, perhaps even blaming her for it all.

But there was no help for it. The commands of the Crown Prince were sacrosanct, to be disobeyed at one's peril.

The fact that she looked exceptionally pretty that afternoon gave Chantra no pleasure. It would have been different had James been the object of her dressing up in silk blouse and embroidered pasin, but at the entertainment they were about to attend the royal children must sit meekly out of the limelight. Only at the end of the display would they be presented to the visitors, filing in procession before the prince and his guests, making their bows, hands held palm to palm in front of their faces in the usual manner, then passing on. She herself would be last of course, after the smallest of the princesses, because she was not the daughter of the Crown Prince, but only his niece.

Miss Bradbury marched them primly from the women's quarters, through the courtyard and out into the sprawling complex of the palace grounds in its enclosing wall. They continued sedately past the splendid home of the White Elephant, to the northern edge of the town. Here, just outside the walls, was the *paniad,* or elephant kraal, a vast place enclosed by a high stockade.

Here, wild elephants, caught in the jungle while still young, were kept and trained. The best-looking and most intelligent were taught to obey commands and eventually walk in procession on state occasions, carrying the Crown Prince and his relatives in style. The remainder were reared in a manner that made them aggressive and ready to fight each other on provocation.

Chantra followed the others to a row of seats immediately behind those reserved for the prince and his guests. They were set on a platform to enable the younger children to see above the heads of the adults.

"Now remember, no fidgeting and no talking," Miss Bradbury cautioned, "or punishment will follow."

Soon after came the prince and his guests, and when they had settled down the entertainment began. At first it was pleasant enough, the more docile animals showing off the tricks they had been taught. Chantra enjoyed this part and applauded with the rest, but when two fighting elephants, their *mahouts* in splendid attire astride their necks, confronted each other in the center of the arena, she closed her eyes.

She knew all too well what would be following. The cruel barbs of the mahouts goading their mounts into activity, the head-on clashes of the two huge beasts, the goring with the great fighting tusks that could cause frightful injuries. Only when one elephant was clearly beaten was the other proclaimed the winner and the wretched creatures allowed to retire, to make way for two fresh combatants.

At last it was over. Miss Bradbury made a sign to her charges to make their exit.

With a sigh of relief, Chantra followed her smallest cousin slowly past the row of guests on either side of the prince. Eyes meekly cast down, they made their abeyances, hands humbly together in front of their faces.

Perhaps she felt the intense scrutiny of the man on the prince's right, for involuntarily her glance flickered upward for a moment to encounter a pair of black eyes, a pockmarked face and an expression of avid desire.

Hastily she lowered her glance. The man must be well over forty and his interest was quite repugnant to her.

But the antipathy was not mutual, for the following morning immediately after breakfast Chantra was sent for to attend the prince in his private apartments.

"Whatever can he want!" Miss Bradbury quavered, apprehensive of displeasure falling on her own head.

As a matter of course, she accompanied her charge to find the prince alone, his guests having left the palace. He came straight to the point of this summons.

"You made a good impression on Prince Prasad Thong, who lives in Chiengmai, far to the north," he began. "The prince lost his wife a few weeks ago, so he is casting around for a replacement of suitable birth. He now feels that he has found her in the form of my niece. As he is rich and prosperous, I consider the match to be a good one, especially as he will demand only a small dowry. I have therefore given my consent to the marriage in eight months' time, when a decent interval of mourning will be over."

Recalling the pockmarked, middle-aged face, Chantra was stunned.

"Why do you not speak? Are you not delighted?" the prince said irritably.

"But he is old and ugly," she stammered.

Her uncle's face darkened. "Who are you to criticize the choice made for you? An orphan with no dowry except what I give you in my generosity. All these years I have kept, clothed and educated you, and this is all the thanks I get!"

"Forgive me," she murmured, fearful that she might be punished by being locked in her room, and so cut off from ever seeing her secret love again.

"Then let me hear no more objections. From now on you will apply yourself to learning all the skills necessary to the wife of an important man and the running of the domestic side of his household."

"It shall be so, my uncle."

The tumult within her belied the meekness of her words. Her budding breasts, which still seemed to feel the touch of her captain's hands, heaved with suppressed emotion. How could she ever contemplate without repugnance the thought of that old pockmarked man mauling them after losing her heart to a being more thrilling than any king?

Miss Bradbury marched her back to the women's quarters, scolding roundly as they went.

"From now on you will take your afternoon siesta with the rest of us, so that I can keep an eye on you," she ended.

This was almost too much to be borne. In a few days Captain James Stuart would be sailing away from the British trading station across the wide ocean to far-off Britain. Voyages were long and hazardous. Before he returned—if ever he did—she would be married to that odious man and living far away from Ayutthaya. It was almost certain that she would never see him again.

But fate decreed otherwise. Two days later, when Chantra felt that life was at its lowest ebb, two of her young cousins went down with a severe attack of typhoid that quite alarmed Miss Bradbury.

"It is quite likely to spread through you all," she lamented, "but you may escape if you isolate yourself in your room, Chantra. I'll get one of the concubines to come and help me nurse the sufferers in the dormitory, and you can pursue your studies alone until I'm at liberty to supervise you again."

Chantra, striving to hide her joy, sent up a profound prayer of thanks to Lord Buddha, who had taken pity on her in this miraculous way. Now she could surely contrive to steal out again and see her captain once more, to explain the situation and bid him farewell before he sailed.

So that afternoon, immediately after a simple lunch in her room, she stole out through the courtyard and gained the outside of the palace unseen. This time there had been none of her cousins' garments around to use as disguise, so she was forced to keep on her give-away pasin of many-colored cotton. However, as so many women paddled themselves around the klongs in small boats, either on selling or buying expeditions, no one was likely to take much notice of her, she reflected as she hired a flat-bottomed punt from the usual source.

It was a beautiful afternoon, with the clouds and mists of the monsoon quite gone and the enervating humidity ended. The sun shone down warmly from the bluest of skies, and the banks of the klong were luscious with teeming new growth.

She poled herself into the broad river and along to the foreign trading stations, her heart beating madly as she approached the one with the British flag aloft. Would he be visible, or had he, after waiting in vain for two days, now given up hope of ever seeing her again.

At first there was no sign of him. Two seamen worked on his ship, whistling cheerfully, but she shrank from drawing their attention to herself in any way. So with her boat drawn up beside the wooden jetty, she sat as quietly as possible, hoping desperately that he would emerge from the wooden building that served as office and living quarters for any ship's officers who happened to be in port.

At last she saw him, but he was not looking her way. He was glancing over toward the ship, shading his eyes from the sun.

She longed to call out, but was too embarrassed by the presence of the seamen to draw their attention her way. Yet she could not let this possibly last opportunity pass and see him turn back into the building without even knowing she was there.

Instinctively she stood up in the boat, staring avidly at him, willing him to look her way and recognize her.

It worked. As though a voice had called, he glanced in her

direction, then, with a suppressed exclamation, strode over and stared down at her.

"It's really you, Chantra! I thought I should never see you again. I've had orders to sail at dawn tomorrow, sooner than expected. Where can we go to talk?"

"Mongkor Wat?"

"Splendid." He stepped down into the boat and took the front seat, facing her this time so that he could watch her pull away from the jetty and the curious gaze of the seamen.

"Now you look sweeter and more desirable than ever, dressed in your normal clothes instead of that boyish disguise," he murmured, feasting his eyes on her as they moved into the current and weaved in and out of the other boats. "You can't imagine how horribly disappointed I felt when you didn't turn up these past days. I imagined all kinds of possibilities, from your being discovered while stealing back and locked in your room, to your having decided you didn't care much for me after all. That was the most galling of all."

"As if I ever could." She was too young and inexperienced to tease him. Her brown eyes and rapt expression betrayed the depths of her infatuation.

His blood quickened. "It's damnable having to leave tomorrow, just as we were getting to know one another. But you haven't yet told me what kept you away."

Her face sobered as she remembered the devastating reality. She said flatly, "I could not escape. There were festivities at the palace that I was forced to attend. They ended in my uncle arranging a marriage for me with one of the guests. I am to be married in eight months' time."

"No!" He looked utterly deflated. At last he said, "What is the lucky man like? Young and good-looking and worthy of you in every way, I hope."

She shook her head. "Middle-aged and widowed and pockmarked, and living in the far north. I shall hate it, but there's no escape."

"My God, what a prospect for you! It's quite damnable my

having to leave tomorrow, or perhaps I could have done something about it."

Smiling, she said, "Nothing, short of your abducting me, can change the decree of the Crown Prince."

"It might even have come to that, given more time."

He convinced neither her nor himself, imagining the reaction of those in authority to such a step, and the snubs she would receive in England from society-at-large, no matter in what capacity he introduced her there.

"If the Lord Buddha decrees it, I must submit," she sighed. "But now, for today, let us forget such a prospect and enjoy our last hours together to the full."

The little wooden shacks with their thatched roofs slid by and finally petered out. They reached Mongkor Wat, hidden away behind the lush river growth, hemmed in and half-grown over by the creeping jungle foliage.

The stillness after the bustle and babel of the klongs was like balm. Only the lizards and the brightly plumed birds shared the solitude and silence.

They wandered among the decay of centuries as they had done that first day, then he said: "I have something for you. A small birthday present. I bought it from one of the silversmiths, and was terribly disappointed at the thought of never being able to give it to you. If we can find somewhere to sit down, I'll give it to you after all."

A sandy hollow, sheltered by broken masonry and a headless Buddha, proved the perfect place. They sank down in its secluded depths.

He pulled off his smart, sweat-streaked tunic and from one of the pockets extracted something done up in tissue paper. On opening, it disclosed a silver filigree necklace set with semiprecious stones mined in the country.

"Oh, it's quite beautiful," she murmured. "I've never owned even a bracelet before. This silver is mined in Siam, you know, as well as the stones. It will be my greatest treasure, but I must keep it hidden."

"At least wear it for me, just while we're together," he urged. "Come, I'll fasten it on myself."

She undid the top button of her shirt and faced him expectantly, and his hands went around her honey-colored neck to secure the pretty thing at the back.

"Now you look more than ever like a princess," he said, his arms still around her shoulders.

"And you more like a prince than any I've seen in Siam," she answered, gazing up into his blue eyes. "If only you were the one I must marry, I should be the happiest girl in all Siam." She sighed, then added, "Why is life so difficult?"

"Sweet child." His voice was husky with the urgent desire that surged through him. How different she was to the few girls he had met in England, with their prim high necklines, tight-laced bodies and coy reactions. As natural and refreshing as a woodland nymph, with her golden face, flimsy drapery and half-revealed bosom, whereon rested his gift. Alone in this sun-drenched paradise, her emotions as turbulent as his, it was too much to expect him to react as he would have done back home.

"I love you more than anyone in the world," he murmured, his mouth drawn magnetically to hers. "Oh God, how I love you and want you."

She said nothing, but her sweet lips parted, her breath coming fast and warm to mingle with his. Her brown eyes closed, the dark lashes lying like a fringe on her cheeks.

His arms tightened, drawing her urgently closer. Her slender body was as soft and pliant as thistledown in his hold. A mist swam before his eyes. An imperative wave of desire surged through him, blotting out everything save his overpowering need.

Without volition they were lying together on the sun-warmed sand, locked in each other's arms. His virile hardness was heaven against her yielding softness, a magical support bringing a strange, warm urge that demanded even closer contact. Inevitably it followed.

Rapture such as she had never known existed filled her. It was like the bursting of a thousand stars in a midnight sky, flashing across the heavens in wave after wave, to slowly die like a falling meteor.

It left her spent, speechless and fulfilled, lying in a half-trance beside him, oblivious of everything save this new delight.

Neither of them spoke for a long time. At last he said ruefully, "I'm sorry. Can you ever forgive me?"

"Forgive you, for showing me Nirvana?" Her voice was a caress.

"But I have to sail away and leave you. We've found heaven, only to lose it again."

She sighed. "At least I shall have a dream to remember all my life. Nothing can take that away, not even when I'm married to someone else."

The thought was even more repugnant to him, now that he had plumbed the depths of her sweetness, but there was nothing he could do about it. Sighing too, he rose. It was time to get back to normal life and sanity. And tomorrow, to England, so far away.

CHAPTER TWO

Six months had passed. The wintertime, with its slightly more tolerable atmosphere, was over. The enervating heat and humidity that preceded the monsoon was upon them, to be endured as best they could.

Chantra had never been so unhappy in all her short life.

One reason was that she had never again seen Captain James Stuart, the man who had burst into her sheltered life like a brilliant meteor. The man who in so short a span of time had changed her life completely.

The consequences were likely to be devastating, she realized with growing terror, for her secret could not be concealed much longer. The nagging fear of discovery haunted her night and day, leaving her listless and on edge.

"I can't think what ails you!" Miss Bradbury scolded. "With your marriage only two months away, and the prospect of going to live in the beautiful north and being a respected wife, you ought to be bubbling over with excitement. But you always were a difficult, ungrateful child."

She realized what the trouble was the day she saw Chantra changing her sweat-streaked pasin for a clean, fresh garment. The slender figure was enlarging in a way that could no longer be hidden. With a shock of horror, the governess saw that Chantra was pregnant.

"You wicked, sly creature!" she shrilled, almost beside herself with rage. "Is this the way you repay my careful upbringing? How do you suppose your uncle is going to react to the news? And even more catastrophic, how can your planned marriage go ahead now? What on earth is your suitor to be told?"

Chantra merely shrugged her slim shoulders. As life was now, she could scarcely care less what happened to her.

But Miss Bradbury was not finished.

"I suppose this is the result of your stealing out while I was kept busy over the typhoid outbreak and you were left to your own devices!" she persisted. "What man bedazzled you to such an extent as to make you no better than a low alley cat?"

"What does it matter now?"

"It matters a great deal, since your uncle will probably punish him and force him to marry you immediately, I suppose it is one of the palace staff with whom you spent those surreptitious afternoons."

"Of course not!" Chantra sounded utterly scornful.

"Who then? You'd better tell me or I'll whip it out of you, since I have the power."

Sooner or later her resistance would be worn down, the girl knew. There seemed no point in trying to hold out, since the British trading post did not come under the rule of this country, and James was far away from condemnation or coercion. It had added to her worry that although she had managed to make several surreptitious visits to the riverside shed, and twice seen a British ship, the captain had not been her secret love but an older man. The voyage to and fro must take far longer than she had realized, or else he must have been transferred to some other route, she concluded.

"I fell in love with a British captain from the river trading post," she confessed at last, "and he with me. I shall never love anyone else, so I don't care if the proposed marriage to that odious northerner does have to be canceled."

"You're a wicked, abandoned creature! This looks worse and worse. Even had the man in question been available and willing, your uncle would never countenance a mixed marriage. As for your planned marriage, words fail me. The problem is beyond me. All I can do is inform your uncle at once and leave the outcome to him."

Chantra cringed inwardly. His wrath could be devastating. Yet no punishment he might conceivably devise could add to her already rock-bottom state, she reflected.

She was wrong, as she found out when Miss Bradbury marched her grimly for a private consultation with the great man.

He listened with stunned disbelief to the governess's story, then stared at his niece with utter loathing.

"There is only one punishment for such flagrant betrayal of my decree," he said, "and that is death. Since the truth cannot be revealed to him and the general public, that is the only way out. I will announce that you are sinking in a decline, which does affect young women from time to time. You will be confined to a locked room, seeing no one except Miss Bradbury for your essential needs. Your prospective bridegroom will be informed that the marriage will not now be possible since you have but a short time to live. That way, neither I nor he will suffer loss of face and be the subjects of vulgar mirth. In a short time you will be given poisoned wine that will end your miserable existence and that of the accursed child. That is the only honorable way out. Do you not agree, Miss Bradbury?"

The governess, afraid for her position and of being considered negligent in her supervision of the girl, reluctantly agreed with him.

He turned a malevolent gaze upon her. "You will swear, on pain of your own death, to breathe no word of this deplorable episode to any living creature, for in some measure you cannot be considered wholly blameless, Miss Bradbury."

"Never, I swear," she quavered, her legs like jelly beneath her at the thought of her own narrow escape, and the stories she had heard of past atrocities meted out by all-powerful despots such as this to those who crossed them in any way. Poisoned food, the sword, an encounter with a cobra, all these and many more devices could be used against victims and their deaths passed off as accidents without a raised eyebrow. It was a brave, or unlucky, being who fell foul of royalty in this land.

"The spire room," the Crown Prince broke in on her fearful reflections. "That is where she will remain hidden until I decide the time is ripe for her to die. You will attend her once only each day, and tell the children and any concerned that she is too ill to be disturbed. Come, I will show you the way myself, for this is too degrading a matter to let anyone else guess the truth."

The spire room. Miss Bradbury had vaguely heard of it as a secret place of confinement for erring or discarded wives, plotting kinsmen who aspired to depose their rulers or any other deemed in need of dire punishment. It was high up in the great central spire, without window or lookout of any kind. Only the Crown Prince knew the secret entry and only he kept the key.

He produced it now, and led the way from his private apartments to a hidden door that gave on to a flimsy spiral staircase winding upward. Round and round and up and up they went until it seemed they must be up in the clouds.

Then her uncle unlocked a small low door and Chantra was thrust inside.

"Reflect on your sins, wanton. By the time death comes, you will be longing for it. That will be your punishment," he said grimly. Then the door was slammed in her face, the key turned in the lock, and she was left alone.

The circular room was so tiny that only a few steps in any direction were possible. It was even narrower at the top, and Chantra could envisage the room as being close to the top of the soaring spire that from below almost seemed to pierce the sky. Having no window, it would have been quite dark, but for a small grating near the ceiling which gave enough light and air to see and breathe.

There was no furniture. Only a couple of old blankets on the floor served as bed and seat, and a pail as a crude toilet device. In silent misery Chantra sank down to contemplate her grisly plight, and with the resilience of youth, presently decided to fight back.

Since there was no knowing how long the Crown Prince would play his cruel cat-and-mouse game before he decided that she had been punished enough and ended it forever, she must try to make the prison more endurable, she concluded. Its worst features were the claustrophobic smallness and the lack of a window through which to catch a glimpse of the world outside. The first could not be remedied, but it was just possible that she could make a brief peephole if she tried.

She scrambled to her feet and circled the confined space, inspecting the walls closely. The structure of this highest part of the spire was of wood which, though doubtless once tough, was now succumbing to the ravages of burning sunshine and drenching monsoon. She saw with satisfaction that it was rotting and crumbling in several places, and in one spot, about a foot above floor level, a tiny beam of light showed that there was actually a small hole.

She knelt down and examined the place with her keen young eyes. The wood was dry and powdery, offering little resistance to the finger she poked through the hole. It required not too great an effort to enlarge it to several inches in circumference, before her hand began to suffer and blood welled from scraped skin.

If only there had been some tool, the growing hole could soon have been knocked into proportions sizable enough to see through. Since the prison room contained nothing more helpful than the blankets, she must make the most of that, she decided.

Wrapping a corner of one firmly around her hand for protection, she again made an onslaught on the hole, managing to enlarge it a little at a time. Her hand soon protested at this rough treatment and she was forced to stop, but only for a while.

Time was the one thing she had plenty of just now, so as soon as her hand had recovered, she set to again with a will. All through the long, hot afternoon she worked, alternately resting and working, until, to her great satisfaction, she had made a hole roughly eighteen inches square.

There was no question of escaping this way, she realized when she thrust her head through the hole and saw the outside world far below, the people like tiny ants. Only space and air surrounded her up here, with no projection below that might form a foothold to climb out on. The very thought of attempting to climb down from this height left her feeling dazed and sick. It would also be useless to try to attract attention to herself by shouting and waving. Even should her voice carry that far down, anyone who located her would simply inform the palace. When the news filtered through to the Crown Prince, his rage would be such that he would execute her at once, and even in these dire circumstances, Chantra did not welcome that contingency. "While there's life, there's hope," was a favorite motto of Miss Bradbury, with which Chantra fervently agreed.

She had just reached this conclusion when a heavy creaking on the winding staircase outside set her panicking. The hole must be kept secret or it might be blocked up again with stronger material. Seizing the two blankets, she piled them in front of the yawning gap, topping them with an armful of musty rice straw that served as a pallet bed. This, together with the now-falling dusk, effectively concealed what she had done from any cursory glance.

There came a turning of the key outside, and then in stepped Miss Bradbury, bearing a tray with food and drink and a few garments hanging over her arm.

"The children are at their supper," she explained, "so I took the opportunity of bringing some for you. I've also brought you a change of clothes and a book to read. It is the English Bible, which will give you some comfort if you study it during the hours of daylight. The Crown Prince would not approve of these, but I am a woman and feel some compassion for you in your unhappy plight."

"Thank you," Chantra said, standing in front of the secret hole to keep the governess's attention from it, though confident that it would not be noticed. "It is kind of you to trouble."

"I can only come once a day at this time," Miss Bradbury explained, "so you must pass the time as best you can. It grieves me that you have brought such calamity on yourself."

She left then, as though fearful of being caught in her magnanimity, and Chantra breathed a sigh of relief when the door was relocked and she was alone again.

She hungrily ate the rice and sauces, but set aside the bread and half the water to sustain her through the following day until evening. Then, making herself as comfortable as she could on the straw, she wrapped herself in the blankets and actually slept until dawn.

A long, monotonous day followed, although the hole she had

made proved a blessing. It not only let in more air and light, but allowed her a limited view of the outside world. If she poked out her head, she could see the ground far below and the blue sky above, which made her cramped prison a little more bearable.

The book proved useful too, although she could only read and understand half the words. She meant to continue the study of written English, instigated by Miss Bradbury, to the bitter end, in the hope that something, somehow, would come like a miracle described in the book to save her from her threatened fate.

As dusk approached, she found herself listening eagerly for the sound of a human voice. Solitary confinement was hard to bear for one so young and active. Wryly, she wondered what James would think, could he know of her plight. He would probably feel like giving the Crown Prince the edge of his sword, before rescuing her and carrying her off, but she knew that was only wishful thinking. Even he would have been powerless against the imperial heir in his own palace.

Yet she had no regrets. Those moments of ecstatic love would live with her forever, regardless of what they cost.

The governess came at last with food. She looked so agitated that Chantra wondered with sinking heart if she brought bad news for herself—the news that the prince had decided the time for her to die had come.

It was nothing so personal, but equally sensational. Refugees from the north had been crowding the klongs all day, fleeing from a great Burmese army that had crossed the border and was forging through the land, looting, burning, killing and destroying all before them. They were believed to be making for Ayutthaya, the capital, to plunder the gold and jeweled Buddhas and the priceless temple ornaments of this celebrated city.

The Crown Prince, she added, was in a state of panic, realizing that his palace, with its many treasures, would be a prime target, and his life and the lives of his family in peril. Siam was in no way equipped to fight such an onslaught, having only a minute and ill-trained army and few weapons. Flight would be the only resort, and in preparation for this event, the prince was gathering together some of his jewelry, with a view to transferring it to the royal barge along with his family, should it become necessary to flee the palace.

"He will make all speed down the Chao Phraya River to the Gulf of Siam, and out to Bang Tak Island," she went on. "The Burmese will never dream of following him there, to such an isolated, undeveloped spot, with no lavish temples or palaces to loot. The prince will take refuge in the unpretentious holiday house he owns there, until the trouble is past."

"What about me?" Chantra asked forlornly.

"Doubtless you are temporarily forgotten, and perhaps for the best. You certainly won't be included in the escape party, so I don't know what will become of you. Now I must go before I'm missed."

Once more locked in, Chantra had more to ponder on now. She scarcely knew whether she would be worse or better off if abandoned here. The Burmese had a ruthless reputation in war, but it was almost certain they would never find her up here in her secret chamber. If she could hold out here until they had plundered and passed on, there might yet be hope for her, but she must have the key to make her escape when it was safe to do so.

Reasoning that she might soon be in desperate need of food and water, she ate only the rice brought in to her, and drank sparingly, again keeping all the bread and half the water in store. Then, as it was too dark to do anything else, she lay down and again managed to sleep until morning.

On rising, she thrust her head through the aperture in the wall and took a keen glance outside. Her field of vision was limited, but as far as she could make out, the city had taken on an air of panic. There were no idlers in sight, sauntering around to admire the palaces and temples, and no saffron-clad monks marching sedately along soliciting food for their begging bowls. The few people who crossed her visionary scope were hurrying klong-ward, bundles or babies on their backs, bent on escape. Boats must be at a premium just now, she reflected, for without roads, the klongs and the great Chao Phraya River were the only means of transit. The majority of people who either could not manage to hire a boat or did not care to abandon their homes must be sitting tight, waiting for whatever fate and the Lord Buddha had in store for them.

And for the moment, that was all she herself could do.

In the early afternoon, when the day was at its warmest and most people normally took a siesta, came a change. From the northern outskirts of the city floated the sounds of many voices and drums and gongs clashing triumphantly. Chantra's lookout faced directly this way, and though she could not see clearly what was happening for the many spires of chedis, monasteries and wats, and ornamental trees in the way, it seemed certain that the Burmese army, sweeping down the river from the north, had now reached the outskirts of the capital itself.

Fear coursed through her. What would happen when they reached the palace? Was this high chamber secret enough to pass undetected? Had the Crown Prince and his family already gone, taking Miss Bradbury with them? If so, her own position was desperate, locked in without means of escape, and no one to bring food or the even more essential water.

Then something even more alarming happened. From the direction of Wat Sri Sanphet, the largest and finest temple in the city, with its three great chedis, gold leaf and priceless jeweled Buddhas, a tongue of flame shot up. This revered structure served as private chapel to the royal family and was within the precincts of the palace grounds. It showed that neither the almost complete circle of three rivers, nor the city walls surrounding Ayutthaya, had proved an effective barrier to the invading horde storming the citadel.

Fire! Chantra's blood ran cold. That was the worst-feared calamity of all in this vulnerable land, with its dry tinder buildings. If the invaders stormed the palace and set fire to it, too, there would be no hope for her, trapped up here.

In her preoccupied agitation, she did not hear the approaching footsteps of the governess. Not until the door was thrust open and the woman burst in did Chantra dare to hope that the Crown Prince had relented and was taking her with them after all.

She was quickly disillusioned.

"I just could not go leaving you trapped up here," Miss Bradbury gabbled. "The Burmese army is actually in the palace vicinity, looting and burning. The prince is loading his small treasures and family on horses to flee to the royal barge. Mercifully it is south of the city with a strong guard of oarsmen on it. I must go or I shall be left behind."

"Let me come down with you. I'll keep hidden until the prince's party has gone," Chantra begged.

The governess looked horrified. "If he so much as suspected I was helping you, he would run his sword through us both! I'll leave you the key, but you must promise not to come down for half an hour. The palace should be deserted by then. Actually, you'll face as great a peril down there as up here with no one to help you and every boat taken by the fleeing citizens. I can only commend you to God and wish you well, knowing the reputation of the Burmese."

There were tears in her eyes as she kissed the girl and thrust the key into her hand, then, turning, dashed through the doorway and slammed the door behind her.

For a moment Chantra was tempted to ignore the governess's plea and follow her down. Then prudence prevailed. The only way out at the bottom of this winding staircase was through the private apartments of the Crown Prince. If he had not yet gone, it would certainly be courting disaster to be seen there. If not for her own sake, she must wait a while for the sake of Miss Bradbury, who had never shown any real unkindness toward her, and was in almost as vulnerable a position.

So Chantra crouched by the hole she had made, her terror growing as the noise of the invaders increased and more tongues of flame shot up from the direction of the Wat Sri Sanphet. She could still not see the enemy for the intervening buildings and trees, but could imagine their next move. As soon as they had finished pillaging and destroying their present target, they would make for the palace, the next-nearest prize.

If she remained hidden up here, she would be safe from attack by them, but afterward would come almost to certain death from choking fumes or flames. Almost any risk was more desirable than that horror.

She steeled herself to patience for about fifteen minutes, then decided that she dare linger no longer. She must get down and out of the palace while there was still time. With the river crowded with fleeing citizens and no boats left, it would be foolish to make off in that direction, she decided. Her only hope was the jungle. That should give effective cover until she had made her escape.

Cautiously, she opened the door and crept down the creaking, winding stairs. It took courage to walk through the short, dark passage at the foot and pass through the secret door into the private apartments of the prince, but she need not have worried. All was as deserted and silent as the grave. He must have gotten clear with his family and jewels, followed by the panicking servants.

Losing no time, she hurried through the sumptuous rooms to the women's quarters, and so out into the courtyard. Now, out in the open, the sound of the onslaught was more audible. It was too close for comfort, and a whiff of acrid smoke, borne on the slight breeze, assailed her nostrils.

She quickened her steps, almost running through the deserted grounds and across the city. The people she encountered were all, like herself, fleeing from the advancing horde, mostly down to the river. Chantra took the opposite direction.

Not until she had reached the cover of the jungle did she pause to catch her breath and plan out her next move.

Her plight was still desperate. Alone, without food or shelter, and with the birth of her child only three months away, what could she do to help herself?

Suddenly she remembered the necklace James had given her. She had kept it hidden on her person these past months, fearing that it would be taken away from her. Now it might prove her salvation.

The jungle, though an effective shield from the perils of the city, was a dangerous place. Cobras slithered through the undergrowth, along with other snakes and noxious insects. Wild beasts roamed, some of them aggressive. To survive, shelter and food must be found quickly, and the necklace should help her obtain them.

North of the city, along the river, was the water market which she had so often visited. Since the Burmese would have had to pass it on their way to Ayutthaya, it was safe to assume that they had ransacked it for food, probably burning the flimsy riverside houses afterward. That did not hold out much hope for her.

But with a ray of hope, she recalled the narrow klong flowing into the river there. It came down through the jungle from a village about two miles off, being the only means of transport the villagers had to the Chao Phraya River and the outside world. If she made her way to that village, some kind-hearted woman might befriend her. Many of the water market refugees must have already fled there, some of them bereaved by the aggressors, no doubt. She could let it be assumed that she herself had lost her husband in the conflict, and so gain sympathy and aid.

It was fatally easy to lose one's way in the overgrown jungle. To avoid this, she skirted the great city, keeping just far enough under cover to feel safe. The sounds of the ravaging horde fell sharply on her ears, while the smoke made her cough and consuming flames shot heavenward, high above the tallest trees.

Had they reached the royal palace yet? She shuddered to think what her fate might have been had she not escaped in time.

With the stricken city left behind, she moved toward the broad river and thankfully joined the rough trail running north alongside it. It was now comparatively easy going, and a brisk walk brought her to the water market.

It was as she had surmised. The place was deserted. The riverside shacks and stalls were smashed and looted, boats overturned, and only a few scrawny fowls and grunting pigs foraged around in the shambles.

Only when she came upon a stray mandarin orange that had fallen from a looted stall did she realize how hungry and thirsty she was. She peeled and ate it, then found several others and ate them, too.

Now refreshed, she pondered her next move. Obviously, it would have to be up the narrow klong to the village, but as it was now dusk, darkness would soon fall. A jungle track would then be fraught with danger, and the few boats left were at the moment

waterlogged. It would be best to spend the night here and move
on in the morning.

A short search revealed one of the houses on stilts with half its
roof remaining. Here she curled up on rice straw in a corner and,
tired from unaccustomed walking, drifted off to sleep.

CHAPTER THREE

Exhausted as she was, Chantra slept well past dawn. The sound of voices roused her. Were the Burmese back, she wondered in panic, then realized the absurdity of this. With the greatest and richest city in all Siam to loot, they would be kept busy for some time yet. Only when sated with plunder and devastation there would they return upriver toward Burma, towing boats laden with loot. Besides, the voices were unmistakably those of her own people, and they came from the direction of the klong flowing out from the jungle.

She rose and hurried from the ruined shack to see half a dozen boats clustered together, the occupants staring half-fearfully at the remains of the village, as though to make sure no enemy lurked there before disembarking.

"All is quiet," Chantra assured them. "The Burmese have passed on to Ayutthaya. They are looting and burning the temples and palaces there."

The people in the boats stared curiously at her, clamoring to know how she had got here.

A little deception was her best course, Chantra decided. It was best to pretend that she was simply an ordinary person like themselves, driven from home and bereft of husband. That way they would be more sympathetic toward her.

"I was very frightened when the Burmese came and started rampaging and burning," she said. "My husband was killed, but I escaped into the jungle and made my way here. I could see the invaders had been here and driven you away, and determined to make my way up the klong and join you today. I'm very glad to see you."

One of the two women in the boats stepped out and took her hand. "It is an evil day for us all. We had a number of our people killed and wounded too. Of course you must take refuge with us. I will look after you, until your child is born."

The second woman, older and with piercing black eyes, followed the other ashore.

"An evil day indeed," she wailed. "What did I predict? The klongs of Ayutthaya will run red with blood. Gold and jewels will be torn from the temples, and gold leaf melted from the Buddhas themselves. Nothing of value will be left. Our great and beautiful capital will be only a shambles, never to recover. Grass will grow in the streets, and creepers cover the ruins, until at last the jungle takes over."

"Do not fret, Mother," one of the men comforted her. "In time it will all be rebuilt as fine as ever."

"Never, never," the crone declared. "A new capital will arise farther down the river, and Ayutthaya will remain a ruin and a legend. I have seen. I have spoken."

"Enough of that!" one of the young men said impatiently. "We came to seek anything we can salvage from our broken homes, not to lament. In time, we shall return here and restore our village again, but that must wait until the enemy has passed back to his own country. Now to work, my friends, to collect what we can. The livestock will be useful if we can catch them."

Then began a lively chasing of fowls and piglets. Some of them were caught and tied in nets. Others escaped into the jungle.

The younger woman in the party, whose name was Jolinda, now took Chantra to what had been her home. The palm-leafed thatched roof had now caved in, but a search among the debris yielded a few household goods. Pots and pans, clothes that belonged to her and her two children, worn towels and a couple of patched blankets. They were covered in dust but welcome finds.

"No rice or other food," Jolinda said sadly. "I expect those devils took it all."

The other items were carried to one of the boats between them, where they found the rest of the party also loading useful objects they had unearthed from the wreckage. There were even a few tools, which the men declared would make the erection of new homes in the jungle village much easier.

"We'll need more boats to transport this lot," they declared, and promptly set to work righting and mopping out any that had not been deliberately smashed by the rampaging army.

Meanwhile, Chantra, feeling quite hungry, went with her new-found friend to a banana grove on the edge of the jungle that the Burmese had overlooked. She ate her fill, drank some water from a spring, then helped Jolinda carry a stem of bananas back to the other members of the party.

Everyone now looked more hopeful and happy. The boats were loaded with all their finds and they set off up the klong to return to the jungle village.

Jolinda told Chantra that she had been widowed a year ago when her husband fell victim to a crocodile while fishing.

"We are two on our own," she added, "so we will team up together in a new house. My children are both under five, and your child will grow up with them. That is, unless you marry again. You are very young and attractive."

"I don't consider that very likely," Chantra assured her, but the other only smiled, with a shake of her head.

The village was soon reached. Here men were already at work constructing houses for the refugees. Long, tough bamboo poles were cut down from the dense bamboo groves and platforms on stilts were constructed by the edge of the klong. From then on it was a simple matter to raise four upright bamboo poles on which to erect a thatched roof. The rear half of these shelters were walled in by matting made from coconut fiber to form a sleeping quarter, while the front half, facing the klong, was left airy and open for healthy living.

Since all the materials needed were free and at hand, even down to the tough liana vines for binding and tying poles, all the houses needed were built in less than a week.

Now she really was one of the klongside dwellers she had always envied, Chantra thought as she helped Jolinda put their new dwelling to right, a simple enough procedure in this place and climate. Furniture was an unknown luxury. They slept on clean rice straw and sat cross-legged on the coco-matting floor for meals. Cooking was done outdoors on charcoal braziers or twig fires, and dishes, clothes and bodies washed in the obliging klong.

Food was no real problem in this backwater either. Rice paddies had been constructed fringing the klong for the benefit of the whole community, as well as an enclosed grove of banana, mango, jack fruit and pomelos. Chantra and Jolinda had also been given a small plot of land on which to grow their own vegetables, pineapples and melons, so, with their few chickens and piglets, they would be virtually self-supporting.

Chantra's baby came easily and naturally into the world, aided only by Jolinda. A beautiful boy, with golden skin and hair as black as his mother's. The only visible feature of his English father were his deep blue eyes, which charmed and mystified all who saw him.

In spite of all the speculation, Chantra kept secret that brief, sweet interlude that had given her this child. Not even to Jolinda did she confide that her supposed husband had been English.

"With a baby so fine and your own grace and beauty, you could almost be a princess," Jolinda said.

"Nothing so grand," Chantra laughed, but thought it prudent to add a version of the truth, to account for her knowledge of English and hands unblemished by field work.

"I did work in the palace of the Crown Prince," she compromised, "waiting on the royal children and their governess. She taught them English and encouraged them to speak it, so I learned quite a lot, too."

Jolinda was vastly impressed. "How exciting, working and living in a palace! What a blessing that the Lord Buddha guided them away to safety in the royal barge. It is said that they are now safe on an island but will return to the mainland one day and found a new capital."

The old soothsayer's prophecy had come true. Ayutthaya was now a devastated ruin, its temples and palaces sacked and burned, its Buddhas broken, fallen and stripped of gold. The Burmese, their dire work complete, had now passed back up the river, their boats heavily laden with loot. Some of the Siamese families were planning to move back to their old homes, restore them and start up the water market again.

"We two, having no man to defend us if trouble comes again, will stay here and grow as much food as we can," Chantra decided. "It is but a short distance down the klong to the great river. We can transport our commodities daily, each in turn, and sell what we can. The other can take care of the children."

Jolinda cheerfully agreed. She was an easygoing, happy, typical Siamese, and the two found that they could live in harmony together. In the course of time, Chantra had offers from several young men of the village, all eager to marry her, but all these were politely refused.

How could she ever take another lover or husband after her wonderful captain? It wasn't that none of the local men measured up to James, but that Chantra was still in love with him. How was he faring these days, she often wondered. Still sailing around the world, no doubt, but never again up the Chao Phraya River to the foreign trading stations of Ayutthaya, for they, along with the great capital, lay devastated and deserted after the raids of the Burmese. No doubt he would conclude that she had perished in the conflict, and remember with nostalgia that sweet interlude in the ruins of Mongkor Wat.

But he had left her one great treasure. His son. Chantra loved him with a devotion that was almost an obsession. She had named him Narai, which was wholly Siamese, while privately deciding that she would keep as much of his English father alive in him as she possibly could.

The child must be taught to write and speak his father's language, of course, and that would be easy enough. She would teach him herself when he was old enough, and perhaps one day he would even voyage out to see that cold, faraway land for himself. He must also have the best education possible. She would work hard, save as much as possible, and send him to the best monastery for a period when he was ten years old. There he would learn wisdom and skills, and later command a fine and respected position among the Siamese people, thus being a credit to his father.

He must be told the story of his father when he was old enough to understand, and keep the secret, she decided. To this end, she wrote the entire episode down in English, in case anything unexpected should strike her down. For this was a land of many tropical diseases, as well as deadly creatures lurking all around, and who could say when Buddha would decree that the time had come for one to pass to the blessed state of Nirvana?

Things worked out as she had planned. Narai grew up a fine youth, tall, strong and of excellent character. His one great sorrow was that his beloved mother died of hepatitis while he was still not twenty and so he was never able to take her away from the jungle village to give her a life of luxury in the new great capital, founded in 1782, farther down the mighty Chao Phraya River, and named Bangkok.

But if Buddha willed it, he must submit, and live his life so that he would be a credit to her and his unknown, blue-eyed father.

CHAPTER FOUR

VEENA 1906

Veena glanced up at the little green lizard scuttling across the ceiling and smiled, wishing she had the same energy. At the moment she felt as limp as the towel on which she was drying her hands.

It had been a busy day at the Mission Clinic in the center of Chiengmai, and even at five-thirty in the evening, the thermometer still stood at eighty-seven degrees. But now, mercifully, she could close up and return to the quiet sanctuary of her small flat, with nothing more demanding than her evening meal to prepare. Father Joseph Flynn had already left, bound for the convent on the other side of town. He was interviewing a novice who was keen to study nursing at the clinic, and hopefully would soon relieve Veena herself.

Not that she disliked the work. It was intensely interesting and rewarding, and Father Joseph delightful to work with. In the three years she had been here, he had taught her a great deal about nursing and as much as he could about simple doctoring, ready for the day when she might be out on her own, visiting the primitive hill tribe villages that at present lacked any help, and where half the children died at birth.

Life there would be rough, Spartan and demanding, if not actually hazardous, for the hill tribes were of mixed decent. Most of the people were more Burmese, Shan and Chinese in their makeup than Siamese. Transport from village to village would be by longboat up the river and creeks, and living accommodation a simple hut with thatched roof, but the prospect held no terrors for Veena.

If she stayed here at the mission clinic much longer, she would be in a rut from which she could not easily break away. A move somewhere must be made soon.

But first a short break would be welcome. Should it be in colorful, sprawling Bangkok, or a dream retreat on the Gulf of Siam, she wondered. With the hot season upon them, the coast would be preferable.

Her speculation was interrupted by a ring on the waiting room bell next door. Surely not another patient. It was after hours, and they must learn to keep within reasonable limits.

But it was not a compatriot that the Siamese porter ushered in, with a shrug of apology, but a tall, suntanned figure who could only be British. His speech confirmed it a moment later. It was in halting Siamese, with a strong British accent.

"I'm sorry to barge in so late. Your porter tells me you are about to close and can see no more patients today. However, I'm hoping you'll take a look at my hand. I've come a long way from an outlying teak camp by boat, and it's darned painful. It needs lancing."

Veena stifled a sigh. Of course she must do what she could for him.

"Do speak in English if it comes more fluently. I speak it almost as well as Siamese," she said. "Now what's the trouble?"

He pulled a soiled strip of rag from his right hand and held it out.

"Had it been the other hand, I could have dealt with it myself without troubling you," he explained. "I've treated many such wounds in my time, but of course I'm not left-handed."

Veena took the hand and studied it. The palm was swollen and inflamed, showing a yellow area of pus near the thumb.

"Jungle thorns?" she asked.

He nodded. "Of course I disinfected it at once, but was too far out for anyone competent enough to remove the thorn. It's still there."

She enlisted the aid of a magnifying glass. "I can see it. Father Joseph, a very experienced doctor, could deal with it more skillfully than I, but he's already left. You have the alternatives of trusting yourself to me, or coming back in the morning."

He grimaced. "I've waited long enough. I'll take my chance with you." His glance lingered on her lovely face, too fair for a true Siamese, especially with her blue eyes, though the heavy blue-black hair was true to type.

She nodded. "The sooner the better, I'd say. Actually, I've been practicing simple operations for some time under Father Joseph's supervision, so I know what I'm doing. This wound had become infected with secondary bacteria, I'm afraid." She was gathering equipment together as she spoke.

"I know. I've seen it happen often enough with elephants, and been forced to repair the damage."

"So you're a vet." She glanced up at him with interest.

He was certainly worth a second look. His thick brown thatch and hazel eyes stood apart from the invariable black hair and brown eyes of her fellow countrymen, as did his height.

"Among other things. I'm a supervisor in charge of a teak concession district. We have to be pretty adaptable, traveling around from camp to camp."

"Oh, then we've treated some of the wives and children from your camps, I expect. They occasionally come in when driven to it, but mostly they're too far off to bother making the journey. We draw the line at elephants, though. Those we'll leave strictly to you."

He laughed, then winced as her probe bit deep.

She pressed him into a chair. "I can deal more comfortably with you if you sit down. We're not used to such giants here."

It was rather a messy business, but presently it was over, his hand neatly bound.

"I'd prefer to take another look at it tomorrow," she said as she tidied up. "That is, if you don't have to get back to the job immediately. The Railway Hotel could put you up no doubt."

"Thanks, but I shan't be dependent on that, since I've a rented bungalow on the outskirts of town. My wife and children live there, while I contrive to snatch a few days there from time to time, between camp rounds."

"Really! If you've been here any length of time I'm surprised I haven't heard of you before. Foreigners are so few they stand out."

"Ah well, this is my second sojourn in Northern Siam and it has lasted only a few months as yet. My first one lasted five years, but that would be before your time. The intervening years I spent in England, where I married, among other things."

"Our country must have made a strong impression on you to draw you back, but it usually does."

"Definitely, but it was mainly the elephants that lured me back. Such lovable, intelligent creatures. Tending pet poodles and cute cats in prim suburbia grew more and more futile, so when the Anglo-Siamese Teak Company offered me the post of camp supervisor, I jumped at the chance."

"It was fortunate that your wife agreed."

"Oh, she was as fed up as I over continual summonses on trivial errands. Siam sounded bewitchingly exotic. She thought it would be a marvelous experience."

"And does she still think so?"

He hesitated. "Shall we say she now realizes the drawbacks," he said at last, "but what situation is perfect?"

"True enough. I'll see you around ten tomorrow morning, then. Father Joseph will be here too. Now tell me your name please for the records."

"David Lancaster."

She stood for a moment after he had gone, staring at the closed door. Trying to visualize the wife who would probably come to hate this strange environment with its enervating heat, torrential rains and incomprehensible language and customs. The wife condemned to suffer isolation and loneliness while her husband traveled around to his lumber camps and beloved elephants. Would their relationship be strong enough to survive?

Someone entering the consulting room from the inner door behind her put an end to her speculations. It was Samrit Udom, the Chinese dispenser, who mixed medicines, pills and potions in the cramped dispensary. She stifled the irritation she felt at this habit of walking in on her without knocking when he knew her to be alone. He did not dare take such liberties when Father Joseph was there.

"Isn't it time you were finished?" he said. "You should keep more strictly to hours, or they'll never respect you. Who was it this time, encroaching on your free time?"

"It was unavoidable, really. He'd traveled a long way from one of the teak camps, and his hand was badly infected. It needed attention right away."

"One of the elephant boys?"

"Oh no. It was the District Supervisor for the Anglo-Siamese Teak Company. I don't think he's been here very long, although he worked for them some years back, he mentioned. His name is David Lancaster."

Udom's eyes narrowed. "That interloper!" he spat out. "How dare they take over the best posts going and treat us like dirt?"

Veena looked astonished.

"What on earth can you mean? You know quite well that all the teak companies employ Europeans in key positions. They have the education, dual languages and veterinary skills necessary for dealing with any emergency they may encounter on their camp rounds, and usually make a good job of it. Siam is extremely dependent on teak and it is essential to our economic growth."

"Of course, but our own people should be given some preference. I myself speak several languages, am educated, and with a little training in the care of elephants, I could do as good a job as any arrogant Englishman. Yet my application was turned down."

She bit her lip. Samrit Udom was ambitious, ruthless and basically without principle. A bad enemy for an unsuspecting foreigner to make. Competent enough at his work, yet she had never liked him. He, on the other hand, lost no opportunity to show her that he liked her quite a lot.

"Perhaps in time opportunities for our people will widen," she said soothingly. "When education is more universal. Our rulers are now more enlightened and we are no longer slaves. With the building of schools and universities, we shall emerge as one of the progressive nations of the East, in addition to our past heritage."

He shrugged impatiently. "Perhaps, when we're too old to care!

Well, to change the subject, let us leave work behind for today.
The porter's waiting to lock up and be off. How about a meal and
a dance show later on? I could call for you around eight."

"Not tonight," she said hastily, trying to think up an excuse.
"I've things to do, like hair washing."

"It looks fine to me. In fact, I couldn't fault you anywhere if I
tried." He glanced appraisingly at her piquant little face, astonish-
ingly blue eyes in this land of brown ones and soft inviting lips.
No doubt it was these pronounced differences in appearance that
attracted him so much.

"Why are you always so evasive," he muttered thickly. "Surely
you know I'm crazy about you and want you strongly enough to
marry you, if I can't have you any other way."

She pulled away from the hands that sought to draw her close,
with a crisp, "This is neither the time nor place for sentiment. As
you've just mentioned, the porter is as eager to lock up as we are,
so shall we go?"

Sulkily he followed her out, and turned away toward his own
residence as she hurried off to her flat.

Father Joseph and the novice from the convent were already
there when she reached the clinic the following morning. He had
the casebook open on his desk.

"I see you had a small emergency operation after I'd left yesterday," he said. "Any problems?"

"None. He exhibited all the stoicism of his British nationality.
The new district supervisor of the Anglo-Siamese Teak Company.
He's living in Chiengmai when not on his camp rounds and is
coming in this morning for a check. You can see him yourself."

Until surgery hour, she busied herself showing the new girl
where everything was and explaining the routine. The girl seemed
intelligent and enthusiastic. She should be just right for the job,
given time and Father Joseph's good training.

David Lancaster was the first patient, with the waiting room
rapidly filling in his wake. In his crisp white shirt and drill slacks,
he looked even more attractive than he had the previous evening,
tired from his long river trip, with garments soiled by perspiration

and dust. The stubble on his chin had been shaved away and his thick brown hair combed into order. He smiled on seeing Veena.

"I hardly think I have need to ask how you feel this morning," she said. "You look much better. Now let me see how the wound is. Father Joseph is here this morning to take a look at it."

She expertly unwound the bandage, swabbing it gently loose where it stuck to the flesh. Father Joseph stared critically at it through thick pebble glasses, then nodded approval.

"As good a job as I could have made myself," he said approvingly. "You do me credit, Veena. If my new assistant turns out as well, I shall be satisfied."

He dressed it himself, then turned the Englishman over to Veena to bandage while he summoned the first of the patient crowd in the waiting room.

"One expects the more enlightened officials in Bangkok to know a few words of English, but I'm surprised to find you speaking it so fluently up here in the remote north of the country," David said as she worked. "I suppose Father Joseph taught you that as well as other skills."

"No. Actually, I've always been able to speak it. My mother knew it as well as Siamese, and passed it on. I'm glad she did now."

"It seems unusual, to say the least, but then, so are you, if you'll pardon the frankness. Blue eyes are uncommon in this country. Could there be British ancestry somewhere back along the line?"

She smiled. "A long way back, but definitely there. Oddly, blue eyes is a dominant heritage passed on. They appear unfailingly in each generation."

"Amazing! They're certainly an asset in your case."

Veena felt her detachment slipping. She became more conscious of his hand, firm and strong beneath the bandage. Never before had her emotions played up in such a fashion when dealing with a patient. But this was no ordinary patient. Hastily she summoned a measure of composure.

She was almost glad to put in the last safety pin.

"Did the accident scare your wife?" she asked to restore her balance.

"A little. Perhaps it was that which brought on her migraine. She's prostrate with it right now."

"I'm sorry to hear it. They can be trying."

"And Selina's usually last three days, unfortunately."

He looked so despondent that she felt bound to help.

"My mother used to suffer from them, so I know how they can upset the whole household. However, I may be able to help. A herbal remedy, which cut short the attacks, was passed on to her by an old friend. I still have the recipe at my flat. I could let you have it this evening if you'd care to try it."

"I guess Selina would try anything that offers help. These frequent bouts are devastating with two young children on her hands, and with me having to leave her alone so often. We have a Siamese couple to help, of course, but they scarcely understand English and the kids play them up. It was like a nuthouse when I had to come out this morning."

That clinched matters for Veena. She could hardly expect him to turn out again that evening for the purpose of calling at her flat, which he might have difficulty in locating.

"Look, I don't mind fetching the herbs myself when I'm through here this evening if that would help you both," she volunteered. "I could show you exactly how to brew them up too."

His brooding eyes lit up. "That's uncommonly kind of you. It would be a great help. I feel so frustrated, not being able to relieve her as I do the elephants."

She took down his address. "Now I must attend the next patient that Father Joseph has just finished examining. I'll see you around six o'clock."

The morning rush took all her attention and energy, but with the midday break came time for thought. There was a small rest room opening off the consulting room, where Father Joseph and his assistants took their lunch, then stretched out on cane divans for the customary siesta. Veena was always glad of the rest, but rarely drifted off to sleep. While Father Joseph gently snored an hour away, her thoughts turned compellingly to David Lancaster and the wife who sounded more of a burden than an asset. Was she pretty or plain, sweet-natured or soured by chronic illness and this unfamiliar, trying environment?

Then it was back to work, on records and case histories and the afternoon session of patients.

Today, she took care to leave with Father Joseph, before Samrit Udom could waylay and pester her. She hurried to her flat, had a hasty cup of tea, then called at a nearby dark little shop on the edge of the klong, kept by a wrinkled old woman, for the herbs grown in the old woman's garden and dried by her.

Armed with these, she made her way to the address given her, walking quickly through streets grown busy again now that the worst heat of the day was over. Very little of the motor traffic that was beginning to filter into the streets of Bangkok was to be seen up here in Chiengmai. Rickshaws still ruled, along with *samlors* pulled by bicycles, bullock carts and similar time-worn devices. Women shuffled along to the pavement markets, poles slung over their shoulders with baskets of produce dangling on either end. Naked children splashed and swam in the klong, while their mothers washed the family clothes and pots. Grain and spices spilled out of sacks from the dark little shops and strange-shaped fruits and vegetables were displayed in front of others.

Then there were the craft shops, outside which the craftsmen sat cross-legged, hammering out the local silver into delicate filigree patterns, painting bamboo bowls and boxes with dark lacquer and bright gold leaf, fashioning gay paper umbrellas or carving teak wooden ornaments. Old family crafts that were handed down from generation to generation, bringing them in a living of sorts.

On the edge of the city she found the bungalow she sought. It was set in a secluded garden bordering the river, and was more imposing than the usual Siamese dwellings, which were open flimsy affairs. Like those, it was set high on stilts to guard against reptiles and insects, and fashioned chiefly from stout bamboo poles, wooden walls and thatched roof, but it was larger, containing several rooms backing on to the open verandah. It also had its own secluded garden behind the bungalow, from which came the sound of childish voices.

Veena climbed the wooden steps and called, "Hullo there, it's the nurse from the clinic. I've brought the migraine remedy I promised."

The flimsy door was opened, revealing David Lancaster, minus shirt, his perfect torso tanned deep brown, the chest hair bleached golden by the sun. His eyes lit up when he saw her.

"You've lost no time. How good of you to bother. Come in and meet Selina, though I doubt if she'll be able to talk much."

Veena followed him through a living room furnished with the bare necessities into a bedroom so shuttered that the woman lying on the bed was only dimly visible. As her eyes adjusted, she saw that the figure was small and slight, with pale, straw-colored hair, and the upper half of the face covered by a shield smelling strongly of menthol.

"Here's the kindly nurse I told you about, my dear," David said. "Her mother suffered the same way as you, so she really understands and hopes to help."

"That's good of her, though I'm beginning to think I'm past aid," mumbled a tired voice from the bed.

"Oh, few of us are ever past aid, at least not before fifty," Veena said cheerfully. "I've brought some herbs which I'll brew up for you. They can't do you any harm, even if they do little good. Now I'll not bother you any more with talking. Just lie quiet and rest until the mixture is ready."

"Rest! Some hope of that with those kids shrieking out there. Can't you control them, David?"

"I'll try. I expect Sam Song's chasing them around the garden. She's as boisterous as they are, but they have been cooped up all day, you know."

He sounded as though it cost him an effort to speak calmly. Selina was no doubt as intolerant and self-centered as many invalids, Veena reflected as she walked back with him through the living room and around the house to the garden at the rear.

It was a good size, but ill-kept. The lawn was bleached by the sun and full of bald patches worn by the feet of two small girls. At the far end was a one-roomed hut which customarily would house the cook and his wife, and attached was the storeroom/kitchen. Cooking was invariably done on a charcoal brazier or oil stove in the open, as Veena well knew, and she would need to enlist the servants' cooperation to prepare her medicine.

"Calm down, you two," David said, ruffling the tousled fair locks of the youngest. "It's almost bedtime, but first you can watch our visitor brew a magic potion to make Mummy better. Fetch water and kettles, Vichet."

Vichet was the cook and shopper, while his wife, Sam Song, did the housework, laundry and kept an eye on the children, Veena gathered. The latter stared at her with interest.

"I'm Veena," she volunteered. "Now tell me your names."

"I'm Vicky, short for Victoria, and I'm six," said the elder importantly, "and this is Sally. She's four."

They were both small replicas of their mother, with the same flaxen hair and wishy-washy pale blue eyes, but they both looked tanned and healthy, whereas Selina would almost certainly be wan and pale, Veena reflected.

They watched with interest as the kettle came to a boil and Veena added various herbs. These she let simmer for five minutes, then strained the liquid off into a jug.

"As soon as it's cool enough, give Selina a wineglassful to sip," she explained. "The herbs should contract the engorged blood vessels in the head, which are the cause of the pain and nausea. They usually bring relief within the hour."

"It sounds like a miracle," he said, taking the jug, "but why don't you stay and see the result for yourself. Have a spot of dinner here while you're waiting. I'm certain you must have come straight here from the clinic without a bite, and it's probably a good way back to wherever you live. It's the least I can do, to offer you a meal, unless you've someone at home waiting impatiently for you."

She shook her head. "I'm all on my own in my little flat, and inclined to take you up on your offer if it won't be any trouble."

"None at all. Vichet is about to cook the most delicious chicken you've ever tasted, while Sam Song puts the kids to bed. In the meantime, come and have a drink on the verandah and watch the world go by on the river."

"Done, if you'll tell me about the teak camps. I've always

thought they must be fascinating places, especially the elephant training centers. We occasionally see one of the women or children in the clinic, if they're in a really bad way. They don't appear to have any medical help, so they're as badly off as the hill tribes."

"True enough." He led the way back to the verandah and settled her in a cane chair. The river at this hour was full of interest. Sellers of fruit, vegetables and many other commodities returning to their homes after a long day in the floating market, families taking a cooling-off before their evening meal, water buffalos bathing and drinking after their day's work. Towering aloft rose the soaring wats of the many temples, high above the palm trees crowding to the water's edge, shading the palm-thatched huts on their cane stilts.

He lit a cigarette and spoke.

"I've often thought it would be a great help to them if some sort of qualified medical or nursing aide could go on circuit around the camps as I do. I supervise the general running of them, and especially the welfare of the elephants, right through their life span. I'm quite prepared to operate on them, but humans are another matter, especially the women of the tribe. Of course, having managed for generations in isolation, they don't expect any outside help, but suffer in silence. I've asked the company if they can't do something about it."

She nodded as she accepted the pineapple drink he handed her.

"Perhaps you'll succeed, but they seem to be an independent lot like the hill tribes. One has to tread warily. How long do elephants normally live, by the way? I've often wondered."

"About the same as us, oddly enough. Eighty is about the limit. We retire them as veterans at seventy, to doze away the remainder of their lives in seclusion."

They sat sipping their drinks until the suffusion of herbs was cool, when Veena took a glassful in to Selina.

"Would you like anything more?" she asked when the last drop was consumed with a shudder of distaste from Selina.

"No, thanks. I may doze off now that the children are in bed."

"The herbs should help there, and I'm sure you'll wake feeling much better. I'm staying to dinner by the way. I hope you don't mind."

"Of course not. David needs the company. I'm no companion in this state, and he sees few cultured people when on circuit. It's his own fault, though. He freely chose to come back."

She sounded as though she herself already regretted it, Veena thought as she turned away with a promise to call in the following evening to see if the remedy had worked.

"I can always obtain more herbs for you," she promised, before softly closing the door on the sufferer.

"She should be all right now until the next attack of migraine," Veena said when she had rejoined David. "Are they very frequent?"

"Unfortunately, yes. I hate having to leave her so much, with only the Siamese couple who speak little English. In Bangkok it would be easier to find someone. Out here in the far north one can't expect it, except for a few educated people such as yourself. If you do know of anyone who'd come and help out, I'd be grateful to hear of them. Any one who would understand her better."

She said without thinking: "I'll be free myself next week. I feel I've been at the clinic long enough. I want a wider field. Traveling around the hill tribes perhaps, if the authorities will back me, but first I need a break. Something to recharge the batteries, you know."

He glanced sharply at her, hope dawning in his warm hazel eyes.

"You wouldn't, I suppose, consider a few weeks here with Selina and the children? Not exactly a rest cure, but much less demanding than that busy clinic, I'll wager. It would be a load off my mind to know they had such competent companionship. You could have outings and picnics together and make a holiday of it. She's seen only a little of Siam beyond Chiengmai. Not speaking the language, she's afraid to venture far afield on her own."

Veena hesitated, pulled two ways. Wanting to help them all, yet chary of getting drawn too deeply into other people's lives. One never knew where such a move would end.

In his earnestness he leaned forward and grasped her hand.

"Do say yes! You'd be under no obligation of course, and could go anytime you wished. Just a friendly arrangement, but of course I should pay you a small salary."

His strong brown hand clasped about her own sent the most extraordinary feeling shooting through her, a sort of warm explosion of brilliant fireworks that shot up her arm and through her entire being. Never having felt such emotion before, she was not quite sure exactly what it was, but knew only that it was quite breathtaking and shatteringly wonderful. Beneath it, prudence melted away. She felt that it would be impossible to refuse his request. She must become part of his household, for a while, and hopefully see more of him.

"I'll certainly consider it." Her voice was oddly breathless, and she could not meet his eyes. "I'll give you my decision tomorrow when I call to see how Selina is," she added. "Will that do?"

"Fine, and do make it yes. Selina will be pleased when I tell her later that she may be having such a charming companion for a while. She gets so depressed, not being able to converse with anyone or go out much, and that of course just adds to the frequency of her migraines."

Soon after, they went into the living room for the meal served up by Vichet. It was the usual fish soup, vegetables, chicken and rice mixture, followed by fresh pineapple, the staple diet of the country, but Veena enjoyed it.

"I ought to be getting back now," she said when the table had been cleared. "Having to rise early, I usually retire early."

He glanced through the mosquito-proofed open window at the thick, warm darkness. Here on the river, all the bustle of daytime activity had now ceased. Beyond an occasional neighbor's voice or waft of subdued music, the night was silent and serene.

"I'll walk part of the way with you if you'll permit," he suggested. "With Selina and the children asleep, there's little to do here and I do need the exercise. I don't get enough while in Chiengmai."

Trying to suppress her feeling of elation, she nodded. "As you wish. This is a fairly law-abiding community, but after dark, one feels safer with an escort."

How strangely exciting it felt to be walking with him through the mysterious night. He was so different from Samrit Udom, whose hand invariably grasped her own, or slid around her slim waist, to her intense irritation. Samrit would insist on treating her as though she belonged exclusively to him, when she had no special liking for him and saw quite enough of him at the clinic.

David Lancaster was another matter. Walking easily and circumspectly beside her, she was still acutely aware of his virile bulk that made her feel small and vulnerable and happy in his protection, as he waved aside a rickshaw boy touting for custom.

"Tell me about your ancestors," he said suddenly. "I'm intrigued to know exactly how you came by those blue eyes and fairer skin."

Veena smiled. "Anyone else might consider it rather shocking, but I'm quite sure you'll understand. Besides, it happened so long ago. Way back in 1767, to be precise. And Chantra was so young and vulnerable. She wrote it all down. The story of her brief, poignant little romance, and the notebook was passed down through her descendents, along with the blue eyes. I have it still, soiled and worn but still decipherable."

He whistled in surprise. "In 1767! This ancestor must have been quite high up the social scale to be able to write at all in those days, and a girl to boot."

Veena nodded. "Chantra was the orphaned cousin of the royal princes and princesses and was brought up with them. A governess taught them to speak and write English, among other things. In her teens she grew restless and rebellious at the thought of her arranged marriage to a much older man. She managed to steal out a few times and became involved with a handsome British captain whose ship was berthed at the East India warehouse on the Chao Phraya River in Ayutthaya. That was the capital in those days, not Bangkok."

"Ah yes. I've read a little about it. The Burmese came and sacked the city, didn't they?"

"Sacked is a mild word. They devastated it so badly that it was considered hopeless to rebuild, so they went downriver and founded the new capital on both banks of the Chao Phraya. A great city, but without the charm of old Ayutthaya, so I believe."

"But surely some ruins are left. I've seen pictures of them."

"Of course. Broken, crumbling mounds, toppled, limbless Buddhas. It is said that the remains have a compelling nostalgia that evoke the past in a most mysterious way. I'd love to see them, especially as that was where my own particular dynasty was founded."

Her voice was wistful, as she thought of that unknown ancestor who had loved and lost, yet miraculously escaped both the wrath of her guardian and the savagery of the Burmese to find solace in a jungle village with her child.

"Then why haven't you? There's a river service of sorts, isn't there?"

"Oh yes, but it's a long way, and I never seem to have had the time. Things are different now, however. I've managed to save enough to take a break, so I just might get my wish."

The night air was suddenly heavy with the scent of frangipani, the exotic temple blossoms that masked an old, crumbling palace. Instinctively, they paused to let the fragrance flow into their inmost beings, bringing a sense of deep peace.

The moonlight lent her an unearthly air; small, darkly beautiful, fey with her contrasting blue eyes. She sensed his attention focused suddenly upon her, and turned away her face because of the pale, drawn face of his wife, sleeping away her troubles.

She began to walk on, saying with an assumed lightness, "I'm almost there now. If you want to turn back, do so by all means."

He ignored the suggestion and paced on beside her until they reached a one-story teakwood house with overhanging thatched roof and a verandah. Beside it stood the spirit house, a tiny replica facing west, wherein dwelt the spirits of the family ancestors.

"I have a room here," she explained. "It isn't bad, but not so pleasant as the river houses, like yours. There's always so much going on around the river and klongs."

"Then change it and come and live with Selina in ours for a while. That way you can save a little more and then have a worthwhile break. Take a really good look at this ruined city of your ancestors." He paused for a moment and then said as though compelled. "I wish I could see it with you, through your eyes."

It was safer to ignore this, she decided, and to put an end to this moonlight stroll, too fraught with undertones, so she only said, "I'll see you tomorrow evening and hope to find your wife better. *Sawadee*, Nai Lancaster." She made the wai, a graceful Siamese gesture of farewell, or greeting, palms together in front of her piquant face.

He laughed. "Why so formal all of a sudden! Good night, Veena, and do make up your mind to come to us for a while."

She was gone, and the night seemed suddenly futile without her. Turning, he strode off to the prosaic domesticity that life by the river had become.

CHAPTER FIVE

"The clinic won't seem the same without you," Father Joseph said on her last day. "However, I agree that the young need to spread their wings and sample as many aspects of life as they can before settling into a groove. I've taught you a good deal and you've been a worthwhile pupil. I'm quite sure you'll do well and spread sunshine and hope wherever you go, my child. Come and visit whenever you wish, and my prayers will go with you."

"I shan't be leaving Chiengmai just yet," Veena reminded him. "A short stay with the Lancasters will give me time to cast about and decide where I can be of most use, besides putting a little heart into Selina Lancaster. She's making heavy weather of life in Siam at the moment. I'll try to get her out and about more, so that she can see what an interesting and beautiful country this really is. It would be a pity if her husband had to give up his job to take her back to England. He's doing good work in the teak industry."

Father Joseph nodded, then called "Come" as a knock sounded on the door. Samrit Udom appeared in view.

"I just wanted to warn you that supplies of quinine are running low," he said to Father Joseph. "Please to put it on order and for calamine lotion also."

"Very good. Now I'll say *sawadee*, Veena, and don't forget to pay us a visit and tell us all about it when you finally decide what to do. The Lancaster bungalow isn't far away," Father Joseph said.

She pressed his extended hand warmly then turned away, hoping to escape while Samrit was with his superior, but to her annoyance he followed her out and grasped her arm, forcibly detaining her.

"So that's where you are going! You know how much I hate these foreigners, and that one in particular, since he filched the post I myself desired from over my head."

She turned to him with annoyance. "Let go my arm, please. You're hurting me. I had no obligation to tell you my plans, since we're not even good friends. If you must know, I'm merely going to spend a short time with his wife and family until I decide on a suitable post. He himself is away on inspection tours most of the time; not that it concerns you."

"It concerns me intensely, and a number of compatriots too. One day maybe we'll be strong enough to assert our will on Lord Taksin Chulasong, Governor of Chiengmai, and force him to change his policy. We Siamese are now capable of running our most important export ourselves."

"Well, I wish you luck, but until that happens, don't pick on those chosen by the governor. That's a mean spirit."

"I can see clearly whose side you are on," he sneered. "I suppose it's that far-back British blood coming out."

She flushed with annoyance. Once, in a weak moment, she had told him the origin of her blue eyes. Now she regretted it.

"Perhaps it is as well that our work will no longer throw us together," she said, turning away. "We could never be real friends."

The following day saw her installed in the bungalow by the river. With David away in Bangkok on business discussions regarding the shipment of teak abroad, Selina was glad to have her.

"Now that the hot season is here, David isn't on his usual circuit," she explained. "The elephants and their mahouts rest for about three months to recuperate for the next working session. Technically, he should have a lot of spare time too, but there's always a number of things to be attended to, he says. It's pretty clear I'm never going to see much of him, so I'm glad to have you, my dear. I'll try to pick up a few words of Siamese while you're here, so that I shan't feel so helpless when trying to shop and so forth. David tried to teach me a little before we came out, but I'm pretty hopeless at languages. He's fairly fluent, since he was here for five years in his early twenties, you know."

"I wonder what made him return to England, since his heart seems to be with Siam and its elephants," Veena said.

"Oh, he grew restless and lonely. There are few English people in the North of Siam, you know. Besides, with talk of the outbreak of the second Boer war in 1899, he felt he might be cut off from home if he didn't get back before the balloon burst. So he came back, met me, and we married in early 1900. He volunteered his services of course and, being a qualified vet, was put to work with the cavalry horses, so never saw any actual fighting, I'm glad to say."

Veena nodded. "I can imagine his frustration when it was all over, and he had to fall back on treating domestic pets."

"Exactly. So when he was offered this post, he jumped at it. Of course, he would have turned it down if I'd been flatly against it, but at the time I was restless too. Siam sounded so exotic that I urged him to go ahead. Edwardian England was rather dull except for the wealthy."

"And now you have doubts?"

"Inevitably, but I'm the anxious type who would find faults anywhere."

Veena nodded. "I'll try to make life a little more interesting for you while I'm here, then maybe you'll settle down better. How about a rickshaw ride this afternoon? There are so many interesting small craft workshops to see. Paper umbrellas, lacquer work, all sorts."

"Oh, lovely! The children will like that too. We'll take a picnic, shall we?"

What was the relationship between Selina and David like, Veena found herself wondering. Being so much apart, perhaps not as close as it should have been. Well, she would soon find out on his return from Bangkok.

The afternoon lived up to its promise. Picnic basket slung on her arm, Veena shepherded them to a rickshaw stand, where the man-powered carriages were lined up in a row. Ignoring the clamor of their owners for custom, she picked out two of the much more modern samlors, propelled by bicycle power, as being faster and more reliable. She climbed into one with Vicky beside her, while Selina and Sally took the other.

A crisp order in Siamese, and they were off through streets comparatively quiet while the luckier townsfolk took their siesta and many of the shops closed for an hour or two.

"Won't the handicraft workshops be closed too?" Selina called from her comfortable seat under its shading hood.

Veena shook her head. Workers were so ill-paid that they were forced to carry on for most of the daylight hours to earn enough for even the most frugal living. Life was hard for the poor, here in the north where few foreign travelers ventured to buy their attractive wares.

The outskirts of the city reached, they bowled along the dusty track past rice paddies now dry and withered in the heat, propelled by the sweating owner of the samlor. The rice paddies gave way to sugarcane plantations. Here, in front of their mean huts, the owners squatted, boiling up extracted juice to make sugar candy and other products which they sold in the city. Veena paused for a moment to purchase a packet of the honey-colored sweetmeat for the children. They squealed with delight on tasting it, and soon emptied the small paper poke.

How gleeful they looked with their sticky fingers and smeared faces. Even Selina had lost her air of passive resignation and was more animated than usual by the time they climbed down from the samlors and began to wander around the complex, where several local handicrafts were carried on. Lacquer-ware, silverware, teak-carving and other crafts were all being carried out by entire families.

How pretty the parasols were, in their delicate shades of rainbow hues, painted with bright flowers. Light and flimsy, they were ideal for warding off the direct rays of the sun. The children of course demanded one each. They were absurdly cheap and Selina passed over the few bahts with a smile. The small girls flitted around with them, looking like gaudy butterflies.

Suddenly the babel of talk among the workers squatting on mats, their fingers moving deftly, died away. All eyes were turned toward a group of people coming into view. A most important party, by the look of things.

Veena stared for a moment. She had seen that majestic personage before, passing in the streets of Chiengmai, being drawn around in his imposing rickshaw by sweating palace servants. It was the governor of the city, Taksin Chulasong, and beside him perched his young daughter, Sawitri.

"Looks like a VIP," Selina murmured.

Veena nodded. "The governor, no less. Khum Taksin Chulasong. He's not quite royal, but near enough. Khum means *lord* in rough translation."

Selina looked impressed. "He's actually handsome, unlike most Siamese," she murmured. "What can he be doing here on a shopping expedition?"

"Probably trying to please his little daughter," Veena reasoned. "He's reputed to be deeply attached to her, owing to a family tragedy. I'll tell you about it later. Little Sawitri is his greatest treasure now, it is said, and since she is rather frail, he guards her with fanatical devotion."

The governor's party, now drawn level with the parasol-makers, halted beside the brilliant display. Veena and Selina lingered with interest, eager to see at close quarters exactly what the great man would buy.

As soon as he stepped down from his rickshaw, the entire population around him made their obeisances in the form of the graceful Siamese wai, hands together high in front of their faces, eyes cast down before this great presence. Veena followed suit. Only Selina, being a *fahrang,* or foreigner, stood awkwardly aloof, gazing with interest at his imposing figure in his flowing satin breeches and gorgeously embroidered tunic.

The little girl, a child of about four years old, jumped down after him, attracted by the pretty parasols. Her eagerness led to disaster. She tripped on a piece of cut bamboo and fell, bumping her forehead.

An attendant darted forward, picked her up and set her on her feet, but Veena, with her trained, perceptive eye, realized that the child was hurt by the rough ground. Blood began to trickle from the abrasion, and tears from the brown eyes.

Somewhat hesitantly she stepped forward, addressing the child's father in their own tongue. "If you will permit me, my lord, I will render first aid. The soil is swarming with germs which could do harm before you are able to return to your palace and have the wound attended to. I have had professional training, and always carry a tube of antiseptic salve around with me for just such contingencies. May I help your daughter, my lord?"

The governor stared at her with piercing dark eyes for a moment, then at the face of his little girl, now smeared with blood and tears.

"You may do what you think necessary," he said stiffly.

Veena whipped the tube of antiseptic from the straw bag she carried, along with a clean white handkerchief. Then, kneeling on the ground before the small figure, she carefully wiped the dust and gore from the wound, liberally applied the salve, and neatly bound the handkerchief around the forehead, tying it behind over the thick black hair.

"That will suffice for the moment, my lord," she said, rising, "but on your return home, it would be wise to have the wound bathed, add more antiseptic and cover again with a clean bandage."

"Of course. It shall be done. No risk must even threaten the health of my remaining dear one," he said, still with a certain stiffness, as though reluctant to become embroiled with a stranger, and a woman to boot. "Accept my thanks for your kindness," he went on, "and if you will call at the palace tomorrow, your handkerchief will be restored to you, freshly laundered."

"It shall be so, my lord," Veena murmured, as he turned away.

The little girl, her spirits restored, now turned her attention to the brilliant display before her, obviously spoiled for choice. The parasol-makers, awed by the presence of her august father, deferentially opened and shut their creations, showing off their allure to the best advantage, each hoping that she would choose his own work.

Finally the child picked out an exotic scarlet parasol, adorned with white flowers and golden butterflies, twirling it above her in great delight. Her father motioned to one of his attendants to pay for it, before mounting into his rickshaw again and being drawn away, his child beside him.

Immediately an excited babel of talk broke out among the workers, honored by such illustrious patronage. No doubt it would serve as a topic of conversation for days.

Veena, Selina and the children moved on toward where the silversmiths sat in a row, laboriously fashioning delicate filigree articles from local mined silver.

"What was the family story you promised to tell me?" Selina asked when they could hear themselves speak.

"Oh yes. It's terribly sad, and caused a wave of shock throughout Chiengmai when it happened, nearly four years ago. Khum Taksin Chulasong was a happily married man with a beautiful young wife and three children. The little girl we've just seen was a small baby then, so mercifully was spared the fate of the others."

Selina's eyes were wide with anticipation. "Whatever happened to them?" she urged.

"Well, in those days, Taksin Chulasong, being a minor branch of royalty, enforced the same rule as the royal family. That was, that no common person should lay hands on any member of the family for any reason whatever. The only exceptions were the governor's valet, his wife's personal maid and the children's nurse. That was the essence of the tragedy, really."

"Do come to the point! I can't wait for the climax," Selina demanded.

"There's a lake in the palace grounds. One hot day, the lady took the two older children, both under five, for a row to cool off. The boat was small so there was only room for the garden boy, besides themselves, to punt them round. Suddenly a large carp swam close to the boat and the surface, looking for scraps of food. The two children leaned too far over the side, throwing out bread and trying to catch the fish. They overbalanced and fell out. The distraught mother leaped in after them, but the lake was deep and with two of them drifting in different directions, she no doubt lost her head. None of them could swim, so there wasn't much hope for them."

"But what about the garden boy in the boat? Surely he could swim and could have rescued some of them at least."

"Remember, there was this strict rule about no common person laying hands on a member of the family. Apparently he tried to save some of them by holding out the punting pole, but this over-turned the boat and he, too, fell into the water. He swam ashore and rushed to the palace to summon help, but by the time Taksin Chulasong reached the lake, his wife and two children were all drowned."

Selina gasped. "No wonder he thinks such a lot of the youngest child. Did he never marry again?"

"No. He mourned the loss too deeply. He even had a marble statue of his wife and the two children sculpted and erected on the brink of the lake. I saw it once when the palace grounds were open to the public. It's quite beautiful. Of course, he changed the law, too."

"What a poignant story. Such a good-looking man, too. It's a shame it had to happen to him."

"I agree." Veena sounded abstracted. She had never seen the governor at such close quarters before, much less spoken to him. The impact had been profound. The deep brown eyes, still reflect-ing past sorrow; the sensitive, reserved countenance, the splendid athletic figure, so superior to most of his fellow countrymen. Fate had dealt him a shattering blow, which even his wealth and posi-tion could not compensate for, and somehow it moved her deeply.

The rest of the day passed pleasantly, and they were all health-ily tired on their return to the riverside bungalow. Here they were in for a surprise. David had returned unexpectedly from Bangkok and, even more exciting, he had planned a visit to the young elephants' training center for the following day.

"I want to see the baby elephants!" Vicky clamored. "May we go too, Daddy?"

David glanced at them all, his eyes lingering on Veena.

"I don't see why not, providing you don't mind roughing it in a bullock cart. That's the only way you could travel. I'll be on horseback, as some of the outlying jungle posts I'll be visiting are inaccessible by any other means. I shall be away for a week or so, but you'd have to return the same day. That would still give you time to see the young elephants being broken in, a most interesting sight. The training center is only about twenty-five kilometers away, so if you can stand the dusty, bumpy ride, I'll take you along."

"Ooh yes, please, Daddy," chorused the children.

"I haven't the heart to refuse them," Selina said indulgently, "although I'll probably regret it."

Veena's heart leaped. "That's sporting of you. I've always wanted to see the elephant training school. With a thick layer of straw in the oxcart and a few cushions, we'll travel tolerably enough."

"It will have to be an early start," David warned, "so get the children off to bed and have a picnic basket packed. I'm sure you'll all enjoy it."

His voice was as gay as Veena suddenly felt. What was happening to her, she wondered. At twenty-two, after years when she had been far too busy and dedicated to the mission work to think seriously about the male sex, nature was suddenly taking over. In the space of a week or two, not one but two men had made a distinct impact on her. But in both cases the choice was unfortunate, for one was already married and the other was too far above her in station to ever contemplate him with anything save awe.

CHAPTER SIX

They were up while the river mist still lingered, before the sun had shown his brassy face. A quick breakfast, then the two women and children settled themselves in the oxcart under the awning, the driver cracked his whip behind his docile team and they were off, with David cantering alongside.

Even so early, there was plenty of traffic on the rough road. Oxcarts piled high with bales of rice straw, or long bamboo poles for construction work, rickshaws and samlors transporting those who could afford the cost into the city, while those who could not trudged on foot, many with bamboo yokes across their shoulders on which were slung baskets of produce for sale. Though much of it went by river, many could not afford the cost of hiring a boat.

"Mercifully, those newfangled motor cars have not penetrated this far," David said. "They'll kick up a most frightful dust if they ever do, but even in Bangkok, I saw very few. Apart from the cost, the Siamese country people are easygoing and tradition-bound."

"But that can hardly be applied to the monarchy," Veena pointed out. "Even a century ago they were encouraging trade with foreign countries, and employing English governesses to teach their daughters and young sons. But the older boys still go to the monasteries to learn obedience, humility and much else from the monks. It seems to work very well."

David nodded. "Yes, they can certainly be termed a go-ahead nation. The governing bodies, from the monarchy down, are doing their best to catch up with the West. One can't say the same for the coolies, I fear, but change is difficult for them."

This was true, Veena reflected, with rice and teak still the backbone of the country's economy. As they made their slow, creaking way over the dusty track and bridges which were merely planks and logs spanning klongs and streams, small rice paddies, surrounded by low dikes to hold the water, covered much of the land. In this dry season the rice farmers were beginning to plough them up with their yoked oxen and primitive ploughs, in readiness for the monsoon rains that would make rice planting possible. There was no lack of interest for passersby, and Selina, especially, was intrigued by these unfamiliar scenes.

As they drew farther away from Chiengmai, these cultivated patches petered out. The landscape grew rougher, with the jungle encroaching in places. Teak and bamboo farm houses, built high on stilts to escape floods and snakes or other obnoxious creatures, were no longer to be seen, and the graceful palm trees and dusty eucalyptus began to give way to teak. Hills rose on every side, wild and desolate, and they passed few people on the rutted track.

"The tribes who live in the hills are poor and keep themselves aloof," Veena explained to Selina. "They only come into Chiengmai when they have commodities for sale. They weave clothes and bags from the wool of their sheep, and dye them attractive colors from natural dyes. They sell quite well and keep the families going, along with their livestock and what they can grow. They're a rough, unsociable lot, but I'm hoping to be able to help the women and children someday."

David looked thoughtful. "There's one crop they grow that causes some problems. Opium. It has been banned by the governor of Chiengmai, but they still grow the poppies secretly. They smoke the residue themselves, and sell a considerable amount of the powder in underhand deals. Too many of the population are becoming addicted to it, so it was made illegal, but that has not stopped it."

Veena nodded. "It's certainly worrying the authorities, and undermining the health of too many. We saw some bad cases at the clinic. Unfortunately, those really responsible for the practice make the money, while the tribesmen, who sell the stuff to them, make very little." She thought of Samrit Udom, the dispenser at the clinic, who had the knowledge and skill to transform the raw opium into saleable products. His father was reputed to strongly encourage the growing of poppies by the hill tribes, and Veena had little doubt that they were in the revolting trade together, and made a considerable amount of money from it.

A wide river now came into view. Here Selina had her first glimpse of the teak industry. Hundreds of great teak logs waited to be transported on their long journey to Bangkok and beyond. Giant-sized rafts of the lashed-together logs floated ponderously downriver, in the charge of boys with long poles who spent weeks on end living on these rafts until they were finally delivered.

"You'll soon see how indispensable elephants are in transporting these logs to the river, assisting in the making of the rafts and in untangling them when the logs and rafts jam," David said enthusiastically. "Elephants love water, are great swimmers and are very intelligent and docile after training. The teak industry couldn't function without them. That's why so much time and money is spent on young elephants in the training schools. It pays off in the end."

Veena smiled. It was heartwarming to see so much enthusiasm for one's work. He obviously loved it, and it would have been a great shame had Selina's ill health forced him to give it up. Fortunately, there was hope for her now.

David caught her glance and smiled back. How attractive he was. A potentially dangerous situation could develop unless she took care. Quite suddenly her heart, dormant for so long, seemed to be galloping off out of control, stirred by every exciting male it encountered. The governor of Chiengmai was another example, and in his case it was even more absurd of her to think of him in any way but deferentially.

Presently David turned his horse into a track leading into the jungle, following the river. The going for the oxcart was even rougher now, so both Veena and Selina were glad when a huge clearing opened out before them and they were able to climb down.

"Where are the elephants?" the children demanded expectantly.

"Just coming. Look across the river."

Sure enough, along a trail on the opposite bank came a slow procession of the creatures of all sizes. The bigger ones all had mahouts astride their necks, while the babies lumbered along beside their mothers or frolicked around with each other.

"Those very young ones just come along to keep their mothers happy and get used to the atmosphere," David explained. "Training starts at about three years old, and most of it is done in the cool season. Today they will just put on a short display to show me how they are progressing, before I make a round of the lumber camps and villages."

The leader of the procession had now reached a spot opposite, where the bank shelved down into the river. She stepped ponderously down and waded in, trumpeting in her excitement as the cool water closed about her thick gray hide. Her mahout slid from her neck into the river beside her, a coconut husk in his hand with which to scrub her down.

"They have their bath every morning, do they?" Selina asked.

"Without fail. They wouldn't begin work without it."

Soon the river pool was full of the great gray bodies, rolling and wallowing, splashing themselves with water from their trunks and obviously enjoying themselves. The mahouts worked dexterously to clean them of caked dust and ticks, while the babies gamboled as mischievously as spring lambs.

The two little girls were enchanted. "We want to ride on their backs," Vicky demanded, jumping up and down in her excitement.

"Presently," her father promised. "First they will show you how they work and how clever they are."

When the mahouts decided that their charges had wallowed enough, they ordered them out of the water and began to prepare all but the babies for training. Working harnesses were fastened around them and chains for hauling logs fixed around their ankles. At the edge of the clearing were stacked teakwood logs of varying sizes, with chains already attached. These were kept permanently on the site, David said, to school the young elephants in the work they would later do in the lumber camps, and get them used to working as a team.

Then followed a most interesting display. The elephants understood the simple words of command of their mahouts, and followed them instantly, dragging logs from one side of the clearing to the other, stacking them up with teamwork, using both trunks and gleaming tusks as levers and lifters. Even the babies took a lively interest in the proceedings, pushing the logs with lowered heads until their interest waned.

After this ritual the intelligent beasts showed their understanding of commands by walking in a single file, forming pairs in procession, helping their mahouts in mounting and dismounting, crouching down on all fours, picking up small objects and other exercises preparing them for the day when they would go out to join a working team.

Now they had their reward in the form of bananas handed out by the mahouts from a pile they had brought with them. The children of course clamored to feed the babies and to their delight were allowed to do so. They were also given a short ride in a *howdah* fixed to an elephant's back, which quite completed their enjoyment.

"I've not enjoyed anything so much for a long time," Veena told David. "Thank you for bringing us. Now I expect you'll have to go off on your rounds while we set off back to Chiengmai."

He gazed at her glowing face, his eyes kindling.

"We could all have lunch together first. Remember the picnic basket," he suggested. "Normally I don't bother with much beyond drinks, then have a good meal in the evening at one of the camps. One of them, where these mahouts live, is quite near. If you would like to see it, we could go there, unless you'd rather eat here?"

The children, watching the elephants depart in procession, pricked up their ears at the thought of following them and seeing a little more of the entertaining beasts.

"Oh, please let us go to the camp," they begged.

"Right, but you'll all have to follow the elephant trail on foot."

He hoisted the picnic basket to his shoulder, then, leaving his horse tethered by the oxcart, they crossed the river beyond the pool on a swaying bridge of flimsy bamboo and ropes, and soon caught up with the slow-moving procession. Quite soon the camp came into view, a collection of simple, bamboo huts on stilts, palm-thatched beneath shading coconut palms, and forming a ring around a clearing. In this clearing a few women, wives of the mahouts, tended cooking pots over fires of teakwood chippings while naked children played in the sunlight.

David set down his basket under a betel-nut tree and Veena promptly began to unpack, until an angry exclamation from him made her look up, to glance in the same direction.

Outside one of the huts, shaded by a coconut palm, a group of about half a dozen young men sat smoking from roughly made wooden pipes. There was a curious detachment about them. They seemed to be in another world, and from the group drifted a distinctive, sickly odor.

"Opium smoking, or I'm a Dutchman!" David muttered angrily. "And it's forbidden both by the government and the teak company. It makes the mahouts too irresponsible and they neglect their duties and the elephants. They obviously didn't expect me coming here today. Not to the camp."

He began to stride toward the group, and Veena followed, as concerned as he. She knew all too well that in spite of the ban, the evil trade still flourished underground, encouraged by unscrupulous men who made large profits in the international markets with opium, heroin and other narcotics. The half-wild hill tribes grew the poppies in their remote fields and sold the crude results for a fraction of their ultimate worth, all too ready to flout authority and help their meager incomes. She also knew the fate of those who became hopelessly hooked on drugs.

The group of smokers stared with their glassy eyes as David approached. Obviously they had not expected this sudden appearance of their supervisor.

"Just what is the meaning of this?" he demanded. "Opium smoking is forbidden while you work for the company, as well you know. Who is responsible for bringing the stuff into the camp?"

There was an uncomfortable silence.

"You'd better speak up or I'll soon get it out of one of the others."

"It was Nai Samrit Udom," one of the group admitted at last.

Then from out of the hut stepped Udom himself, his face set in a scowl.

"What is all the commotion?" he asked cooly. "Why all the fuss over a harmless pleasure? These poor devils have little else to pass the time with, cut off in these camps. Who are you, a *fahrang*, to forbid it?"

"The company and the government forbid it, as well you know," David said dourly. "It saps the strength and makes them apathetic and unfit. They would have little time for such indulgences if they carried out their duties properly."

Udom spat contemptuously. "The company! A bunch of fahrangs who are wresting Siam's resources from her and giving as little as they can in return. Bringing in men like you to run the teak business instead of appointing our own people. You know nothing of our needs and background. Opium poppies have been grown for centuries and its products, along with betel nuts, eased the hunger and boredom of the poor for generations. Neither you nor your company are ever going to stamp it out, I can tell you."

"Not while skunks like you and your father undermine our authority by secretly pushing the stuff at them, but we'll have a damned good try. Get out of this camp and never let me see or hear of your presence here again, or I'll take more positive action against you."

Udom spat again, then turned his inscrutable eyes toward Veena. His expression was so full of venom that she had difficulty in suppressing a shudder. Here was an enemy to be feared, not only by David but also by herself, now that she had openly allied herself with him and his family. An enemy who would work with secret malice to bring misfortune on them, if he possibly could.

"So be it," he said enigmatically, then stalked away toward the river where, no doubt, his boat was moored.

The picnic that followed, which could have been so pleasant, fell flat. Only the children's enjoyment seemed unclouded. Afterward, instead of looking around as intended, Veena and Selina were glad to make their way back to where their oxcart waited, while David remained to give a dressing-down to the transgressors and inspect the elephant quarters and animals to make sure that all was well.

CHAPTER SEVEN

These early morning hours were the best time of day, Veena reflected, gazing out over the broad Ping River on which traffic was already building up. Boats piled high with produce, poled by women in their great flat hats, loomed out of the mist like ghosts. From the floating houses across the water came sounds that indicated the families were up and deep into their morning chores. Women with babies strapped to their backs were washing the family clothes, children shouted and laughed as they splashed about and men set lines and nets to catch fish.

She turned back to the garden with a smile. Chiengmai was a pleasant place in which to live. Slightly cooler, even in the hot season, than Bangkok, five hundred miles to the south. Life went at a slower pace among these remote northern hills and rich teak forests.

Was David still at the camp, endeavoring to put the fear of Buddha into the opium smokers? It was a lonely life for him, traveling around for weeks at a time without a glimpse of Selina or the children, and yet he had chosen to return to it from England.

Here was Vichet, emerging from his garden hut to get breakfast under way.

"*Saw-a-dee,*" Veena called. "I think we'll start with mango this morning. Do you have any?"

He indicated yes with a wide smile and a nod of his dark head. She left him to get on with it and went inside to help the children dress.

They had scarcely finished breakfast when a messenger arrived. "Who can be calling so early?" Selina wondered.

Her wonder turned to amazement when the messenger said he was sent by the governor of Chiengmai to command Miss Veena Basche to appear at his palace at ten o'clock.

"What can he want, and how does he know my name?" Veena said, biting her lip.

The messenger shrugged his slim shoulders. "As to how he knows who you are, that was easy. After your assistance to the child the day before yesterday, he suspected that you were trained at the clinic and sent me there to make inquiries. They said you had recently left, and gave me this address. You were not at home when I was sent yesterday, so I was sent again today."

"I see." Veena turned to Selina. "Probably he wants me to take another look at the child's forehead. Being so attached to her, he'll no doubt be unduly anxious about her."

The messenger left, and in view of the grandeur of her venue, Veena put on a clean blue pasin and white blouse. The pasin accentuated the blue of her eyes, giving her elfin face beneath its mop of black curls a piquant charm.

"It isn't too far to the governor's palace. I can easily walk at this time of morning," she told Selina. "I don't suppose I'll be kept long, and then we'll think up something nice to do this afternoon. I've often wondered what it was like inside. Now at last I'll see for myself."

With quick, light steps she set off. Now the city was at its busiest. Tiny dark shops had opened up, their wares spilling out onto the dusty sidewalk. In the midst of them sat their owners, cross-legged and motionless in the lotus pose, chewing the betel nuts that stained their lips and tongues bright red. It dulled their appetites and had a soothing effect which made inactivity and boredom tolerable.

The crumbling walls and remains of the moat that had formerly enclosed the old city loomed up. She crossed the bridge and passed through the Tapae Gate, to continue smartly along Ratchadamnden Road. Graceful spires of wats rose all around, but she did not slacken her pace until she reached the grounds of the Wat

Phra Singh, the finest of the temples within this complex. Then she walked less quickly, reveling in the peace and tranquillity of the compound and reading the quaint mottoes tacked up on some of the trees for the improvement of the mind.

"He that walketh with wise men shall be wise."
"Fatigue is the best pillow."
"Courtesy costs nothing."
"Hope is the poor man's bread."

There were many more, placed there by the monks. This wat housed a school for Buddhist studies, and young men came from all over the north to gain merit and improve their minds. She could see the bright orange robes of some of them as she neared the fine old building.

Past the temple complex she turned up a side track that led to the palace of the governor. This was a much newer structure, built specially for the governors of the city, and much less grand than the ancient King's Palace, sited outside the city on the road to Wat Doi Suthep.

The building soon confronted her, as graceful as most Siamese palaces and temples with its many-gabled pointed roofs and central spire. The red and gold embellishments of these were beautifully highlighted by the pure white walls and marble steps of the entrance, while to the side lay the lake, dotted by pink and white lotus blossoms.

The lake drew her irresistibly. Now that she had seen the proud, remote face of the governor close to, his eyes still haunted by the tragedy that had shattered his life, she felt impelled to take another glance at the statue on the shore. She had seen it only once before when the grounds had been open to the public for the celebration of one of the numerous religious festivals.

She stole across and stood for a moment, gazing with rising emotion at the beautiful creation. The sculptor had captured unerringly the smiling face of the young mother, one child in her arms, another child at her skirts.

How had he survived the devastating blow? The long, empty days that followed? Small wonder that he now idolized the only fragment of his young wife left to him—the little girl who had been safely at home in her baby basket when the tragedy struck.

This reminded her of his summons, and that he might be waiting with growing impatience. She brushed away the moisture from her eyes and hurried back to the palace entrance.

Two fierce-looking demons stood one on either side of the steps as was the custom in important Siamese buildings. With some hesitation she mounted, wondering if she ought to remove her shoes as one did at temple gates.

The ornate door was closed. She set the dangling bell in motion. The door was opened almost immediately by a guard who must have been lurking just inside.

"The governor summoned me to appear before him this morning," Veena explained.

"Your name, please."

"Miss Veena Basche."

"You are expected. Please follow me."

Feeling slightly nervous, she crossed the entrance hall in his wake. Through an open door she caught a glimpse of the audience hall, a large, ornate chamber where the governor held various functions and meetings. The crimson carpet, golden throne surmounted by its tiered umbrella, and splendid ceiling did nothing to ease her tension. Here was a man descended from royalty, she realized, even though he bore no title of prince because of the numerous offspring of past monarchs.

The guide strode on down a long corridor to the suite of rooms at the rear of the palace where the governor resided. These were slightly less ornate and formal than those at the front, she noticed, as the guide halted and knocked on a carved teak door with the cane he carried.

At his command she removed her sandals.

A voice called, "Enter." The door was opened. Veena was motioned through and found herself looking at the man held in awe and respect by all the people of Chiengmai.

Here in his natural setting, he was even more handsome than she had thought two days ago, she realized. The midnight-blue satin tunic embossed with gold above the amply cut calf-length

breeches and gold-embossed slippers sat with dignity on his athletic frame, so different from most of his contemporaries. His features were more angular than most of his contemporaries, giving
him a distinctly virile appearance calculated to quicken the pulse
of any woman. Veena was no exception as she brought her palms
together in front of her face and bowed her head in deference.

He returned the wai, hands held much lower because of the
difference in status, then said in English: "You speak English almost as well as Siamese, Father Joseph informed me."

"That is true, my lord."

"You are also an experienced and skilled nurse, and very understanding with children, I am told."

So he had visited the clinic and made extensive inquiries regarding her, she reflected as she assented. Why?

"You strike me as the very person I am looking for," he eluci-
dated. "As you have perhaps heard, it is usual for noble families
in Siam to employ English governesses, for we realize the importance of the Western language in world commerce and communications. However, my daughter Sawitri is but four years old, small
and delicate for her age. She is also very precious to me. The
person to whom I entrust her well-being and early education for
the next few years must have exceptional qualities. You, I believe,
have these qualities."

"That is generous of you, my lord," she murmured.

"You will therefore take up residence here immediately and
begin your duties."

Veena gasped. The arbitrary command was well-calculated to
raise her hackles and bring rebellion, but in this instance she
dared not give vent to it. Apart from her own position, there was
Father Joseph and the clinic to consider. The governor of Chiengmai was a prime supporter of this voluntary effort. Without the
generous amounts contributed regularly by him, the organization
could never survive. Even if she disregarded her own safety, she
could not let down the great-hearted man who had done so much
for her these past years.

"You are merely marking time at the home of one of our British teak organization supervisors, are you not?" There was a touch of impatience in his tone at her silence.

"That is so. Mrs. Lancaster is delicate, and glad of my help until she becomes more used to our country. Later on, I had hoped to be able to help the hill tribes in some way. The infant mortality rate is very high in those remote parts."

"All very admirable, Miss Basche, but at the moment my child is more important than a score of infants whose parents breed like flies."

His arrogance was like a red rag to a bull. Only by reminding herself of his appalling tragedy could she quell her rising rebellion.

"So you will collect your possessions and report back here this afternoon."

There was no answer to such a direct order except to bow her head in submission. In this day and age of 1906, Siam was just emerging from an absolute monarchy. Even distant connections, especially if they were governors of regions as important as Chiengmai, were extremely powerful. They could make or break a subject at will.

"If you give of your best here at my palace," he went on in a slightly less austere tone, "I shall look with favor on your future hopes and do what is possible to assist you. I shall also show my gratitude to Father Joseph in practical terms. His clinic does much good work."

"Thank you, my lord."

There was nothing else she could say or do. With mixed feelings, she bowed her head, gave the wai of respect and farewell, and left him.

Walking back through the old town, she noticed little of the bustle around her. Her mind was too chaotic. How dismayed Selina and the children would be at her abrupt departure. She felt she would be letting them all down, and David too.

What would life at the palace be like? In spite of all, excitement surged through her. Surely it was an honor to be chosen as nurse-governess to so treasured a child. A responsibility too, but a challenge she must accept without option.

"So we meet again, my fickle one. And how are you faring in the house of the fahrang interloper?"

At the sound of the mocking voice she glanced up, to encounter the face of Samrit Udom, staring intently at her.

"Decidedly well, though I hardly see that it is any business of yours," Veena said stiffly. "How are things at the clinic?"

Udom smiled in sneering fashion. "We get along, even without your presence, strange as it may seem. The new assistant is learning fast. Moreover, she does not spurn my help nor my advances as you did."

"Then we're all happy."

"But for how long will yours last? What has become of the fine ambitions you once cherished? To work among and help the hill tribes. Had you remained a friend of mine, I could have helped you greatly. Remember, my father lives in their midst and has great influence. He could have smoothed your path and guaranteed your safety in the most remote villages."

True enough, she reflected. The elder Udom lived among them not to aid them but for what he could get out of it. His greedy mind was centered on the opium poppies grown in secret fields. After two or three harvests the fields were ploughed up and the poppy seeds set elsewhere to minimize detection. The elder Udom was the driving force behind the venture, paying the hill farmers as little as possible and reaping large profits from international agencies that bought both raw and refined end products. This was where Samrit, with his pharmaceutical training, came in. Doubtless, he had a private laboratory somewhere that turned out quantities of pernicious drugs. Drugs that in the wrong hands were the ruination of many a young life. These things were never openly spoken of, but below the surface, many people were uneasily aware of the dark shadow lurking in the hill country round Chiengmai.

"You do not answer," Samrit went on. "Perhaps you secretly already regret throwing away your chances. However, if you still desire to work among the hill tribes, you have only to turn to me again. I can help you far more in that direction than anyone."

"You flatter yourself." Veena suddenly recalled what the governor had said about helping her work in the course of time. "I shall have all the help necessary when I need it, I fancy."

"From whom?"

"From the governor of Chiengmai."

Samrit's laugh was derisory. "You must have taken leave of your senses! The governor cannot even know you exist."

"On the contrary, I have just left the palace, to which I was summoned by him. Moreover, I return this afternoon to take up residence there." For the life of her she could not stifle the note of satisfaction as she saw his mouth gape in astonishment.

He rallied, summoning his venom again. "So the governor is taking a concubine at last, is he? Congratulations on catching his fancy, but remember, it won't last. As soon as he decides to marry again, your fate could be most unpleasant."

Veena flushed scarlet. "Why do I waste time speaking to such an evil-minded creature! Find out for yourself why I'm going to the palace. I want nothing more to do with you."

Head high, she marched off. From now on, his enmity would be directed against her, as it was already against David Lancaster. Well, he could scarcely do her any mischief while she resided in the palace under the protection of the governor himself. David was another matter, riding off alone into remote places as he did.

As she had anticipated, Selina and the children were dismayed at the news that she must leave at once for the palace.

"Is there no way you can get out of it?" Selina asked.

"None, I'm afraid. The governor's word is law in Chiengmai. He is answerable only to the King himself in Bangkok, five hundred miles away. But don't be too upset. I shall still be quite near, you know. Surely I'll have some time to myself and then I can come and take tea with you. When I've settled down there, I may ask permission for you to visit me, and show you around the palace. You would like that, wouldn't you?"

"Oh yes!" the children enthused, and even Selina brightened a little at the idea.

So after lunch Veena packed her clothes, ordered a samlor for transport and said *sawadee*.

"Explain the situation to David on his return," she said. "I'm sorry to go while he's away, but it can't be helped. Oh, and tell him to beware of Samrit Udom. He's quite unscrupulous and a ruthless enemy. He has it in for me, too, now that I've shown him what I really think of him, but I'll be out of his reach at the palace I fancy."

Suddenly the prospect of taking up residence there was becoming more alluring. Was it the notion of living in luxury, or the hope of aid with her future ambition, or what?

The commanding figure and handsome face of the governor floated through her mind as she climbed into the samlor. Surely *he* could not be the draw. It was too absurd to think of him in any way save as an exalted employer.

As for Udom's outrageous assumption, it brought a rosy flush for the second time, and now she could not dismiss the notion so scornfully.

CHAPTER EIGHT

The governor's palace had two faces, Veena found on taking up residence there. The front façade, no doubt to impress his subjects, was as lavishly and fantastically fashioned and decorated as most Siamese buildings of note, while the secluded rear apartments had been influenced somewhat by Western ideas. Although the tables and divans were quite low still, much of the ornate carving, hangings and ornaments had been removed, even in the governor's private apartments.

As for the suite to be occupied by Veena and little Sawitri, Veena found to her satisfaction that she was to be given some say in the furnishing of part of it at least.

"Until now," Khum Taksin Chulasong explained as he led her around with his daughter in tow, "Sawitri has been cared for by Nada, a loyal servant who has been with the family for ten years. Since my late wife was taken from us, Nada has had full charge of her, but now I realize it is time for a change. The child needs a more cultured person who can help her with her English, teach her the rudiments of other subjects she should know something of and generally prepare her for more formal schooling in two or three years' time. From what Father Joseph told me, I know that you are ideal for this task, so I shall leave you to arrange your daily program as you think fit. There are few educated females in Chiengmai who speak both Siamese and English."

Veena murmured her thanks as he opened a door.

"This is the bedchamber used by Nada and Sawitri. From now on it will be yours. The child's bed has been moved to a smaller

room through the connecting door, and Nada given a room elsewhere. She will wait on you and do your bidding."

All very satisfactory, Veena reflected, except for the probable
reaction from the unknown Nada. Unless she was exceptionally
forbearing, jealousy of the usurper who had supplanted her was
bound to arise, to make life uncomfortable.

Taksin Chulasong then showed her an adjoining room that had
been used as a day nursery, suggesting that it could now be used
for lessons and indoor leisure. Opening onto the private courtyard, it was ideal for the purpose.

"If you give me a list of any changes you would like made in
the furnishings, I will have it attended to tomorrow," he promised.

Better and better. A small desk and chair would be very helpful
for Sawitri, and a larger one for herself. Also reading, writing and
drawing books, pens, crayons and paints. Veena found herself
warming to her coming task and her new employer as she made a
mental note of requirements.

A utility room where they could bathe, wash clothes and do
sundry small tasks completed the suite, which, like the other
rooms, looked out onto the small, enclosed courtyard complete
with fountain and flowering shrubs.

"You approve? You think you can be happy here?" The dark
eyes that gazed challengingly into her blue ones held a lurking
sorrow that belied the autocracy of his countenance.

"Why assuredly, my lord. You have thought of everything."

It would be a pleasure as well as a duty to make things run
smoothly and do her best for the motherless child and the man
who had so much in worldly terms, yet had suffered such a griev-
ous personal blow. She found herself warming to both of them
and feeling growing enthusiasm for the life ahead.

When he strode away, she turned to his little daughter. How
appealing she looked, with her delicate little face, black curls and
richly embroidered pasin and jacket.

"Have you had your afternoon rest?" Veena asked with a smile.

Sawitri nodded. "Nada always makes me lie down for hours,
but today I was allowed to get up to meet you. I no longer like

Nada. She treats me like a baby and seldom lets me out of her sight. I want to play in the courtyard and be taken out to see the outside world, as Father took me the other day." Her grave little face was full of yearning.

"Well, from now on that will be possible. As I'm to have charge of you, you'll no longer be governed by what Nada says. Put on your shady hat and we'll go outside now, shall we?"

The worst of the sun's heat had passed. In the courtyard, with its cooling fountain and brilliantly colored shrubs, it was now tolerable. Sawitri ran happily to the spirit house, a beautifully fashioned miniature temple standing on a pole, and no bigger than a doll's house. She fished from her pocket a wrapped piece of candy made from sugar cane, and standing on tiptoe, placed it among the rice and other offerings in the open portal.

"What are you thanking the spirits for?" Veena asked.

"For you coming. You are so pretty and young. Not like Nada, who no longer wants to walk or run or play, but just sit and doze when she is not working."

"We all come to it in time." But it was not good for a young child to have no other company. How sad that her brothers had been drowned with their mother. Sawitri needed the stimulation and companionship of other children to develop normally.

Suddenly Veena remembered Selina's children. Vicky and Sally, at six and four respectively, were just the age for Sawitri. Selina would be concerned about their education, now that she herself had been whisked away to the palace. The ideal solution would be for them to come two or three mornings a week and take lessons with the governor's child. That is, if he were agreeable to the arrangement.

"How would you like two little English girls to come and share lessons with you?" she asked impulsively. "That way they would be much more fun. You could help them with Siamese ways and speech, while they would be a great help with your English, although you already speak it quite well."

"That is because Father and I usually speak it to each other. He says it is important now that our country is having more and more contact with the West. I should like very much to have the little English girls for friends."

"Then I'll speak to your father at the first opportunity. By the way, who is that peering at us from the schoolroom?"

"Oh, that is Nada. She looks quite cross but she won't dare scold me with you here." Sawitri laughed impishly.

Veena walked across to the doorway in which the woman lurked. Small, wizened and gray, she could have been any age between forty and sixty in this land where the peasant stock aged prematurely. Her dark blue pasin and white blouse were neat and spotless, but her expression was clouded by suspicion and hostility.

"Come and join us in the courtyard if you wish," Veena invited. "I'm here to take charge of Sawitri and her lessons, but you'll still have your part to play in waiting on her. I'll do my best to see that everything goes harmoniously and hope we'll be friends."

Nada shook her head. "The courtyard is not good in the afternoon sun. I have no wish to come out, and Miss Sawitri should not be out either."

"Oh, I'm sure she'll come to no harm in her shady hat. In any case, we won't be staying out long. Perhaps you'll make us a refreshing brew of tea for when we come in. While at the clinic I acquired a taste for it and find it very good."

Nada muttered something below her breath, obviously pouring scorn on this foreign habit, acquired from the West, then turned away.

"She doesn't seem to think much of tea," Veena said.

Sawitri smiled. "No, she would rather smoke her old pipe. It brings pleasant dreams, she says."

So Nada was an opium smoker. Did Taksin Chulasong know? It was well known that he was trying to stamp out the pernicious habit which harmed too many people, and to discourage the growing of poppies in his own remote province.

The chance to speak to the governor regarding company for Sawitri during her lessons came next morning, while Veena was superintending the rearrangement of the schoolroom with the new desks that had been knocked up overnight by local carpenters.

He strode in and looked round, smiling his approval at the plain, sturdy desks and other aids to learning.

"Everything is as you wish, Miss Basche?" The brooding glance turned upon her sent a surge of awareness coursing through her as she stacked gaily colored picture books on a shelf. "Is there anything further that you need?"

"A globe of the world would be a great asset, my lord, so that Sawitri would understand the position of Siam in relation to all the other countries. That is if such a thing exists in Chiengmai."

"You shall have it as soon as one can be located."

Why did he stare so intently? She could feel it even though her eyes were cast down on the books which she fingered nervously. Her embarrassment almost cost her the chance to put her second request, but Sawitri grasped his hand and piped out. "Oh, Father, I may have the fahrang children to take lessons with me, may I not?"

"What is this, Miss Basche?"

"My lord, I consider Sawitri needs the stimulation of contact with other children. As you are aware, I was living in the home of David Lancaster and his wife Selina when you sent for me, helping with his two small daughters. It seems to me it would be an excellent plan to have them here two or three mornings a week to take lessons with Sawitri. The child would benefit greatly from their company."

He nodded approval. "Mr. Lancaster I know slightly. He is supervisor of the teak camps in the Chiengmai area, is he not? An admirable type and well thought of. I consider your suggestion a good one, so go ahead with it. I had better order two further desks as well as the globe."

"That is most kind of you, my lord." It was gratifying in this city, so far from Bangkok and its changing Western outlook, to come up against an employer with so advanced and tolerant a mind, especially in regard to a girl child. But of course the circumstances were poignantly unusual. Having been deprived of wife and sons in one stunning catastrophe, his whole affections were now pinpointed on his remaining child. Nothing was too good for her.

With some misgiving, Veena suddenly realized the enormity of her responsibility. If anything should happen to Sawitri, it would go hard with her father. And with herself, for allowing it to happen.

"I should like to call on Selina Lancaster sometime today to discuss arrangements for the children," Veena said. "Have I your permission to take Sawitri with me?"

"Please, Father!"

How could he resist the child's eager face.

"As you wish. Outings will be at your discretion, Miss Basche, although on occasion I may have my own ideas and join in. I shall also make time to drop in on you most mornings and see how the schooling is going."

"You will always be welcome in the schoolroom, my lord."

Veena cast down her glance in an effort to mask the quickening of her pulse. Was his interest entirely on the child's behalf, even though his intent dark eyes were fixed on herself?

It was almost a relief when he turned abruptly and strode away.

As soon as the new possessions were settled to her liking, Veena set off with the child for the Lancaster bungalow, resolved to walk one way and return by samlor. The exercise and fresh air would benefit Sawitri, who looked none too robust, and the sights add interest. She had been cooped up too long with the aging Nada.

Selina and the children were delighted to see them. The governor's child was smaller and slighter than her English contemporaries, in common with most of her race, in spite of the fact that her father was one of the few exceptions. Some quirk of nature had made him quite tall. A man to tower over a woman and thrill her with his masculinity.

What Sawitri lacked in stature, however, was compensated for by an agile intellect and an outlook on life far more mature than her years warranted. The result, no doubt, of exclusive contact with adults. Children of her own age were precisely what she needed to provide the element so sadly lacking previously. With great satisfaction, she watched Vicky and Sally fingering Sawitri's beautiful satin pasin as questions tumbled nonstop from them, to be answered readily by the smiling Siamese girl.

"How nice of you to come visiting so soon and to bring your little charge along," Selina enthused. "The children and I have been terribly despondent since you were torn away from us, especially with David away."

They were even more excited when Veena explained the purpose of her visit. "That will solve my greatest problem of how to get a smattering of education for the children in this God-forsaken outpost!" Selina declared. "The governor must be a man of real understanding, and of course we've already discovered what an absolute treasure you are, my dear."

It was decided that Vicky and Sally should come to the palace three mornings a week by samlor. Sam Song should accompany them at first, returning immediately to the bungalow to get on with her work.

"I'll return them by the same means around midday, so they'll be safely back before the worst heat of the day," Veena promised.

The three children, racing like puppies around the compound, were loath to break up when the time came for departure. Noting Sawitri's dust-stained clothing, Veena decided to find her some more suitable garments for playing in, at least for mornings. Something less impeding than the clinging, ankle-length pasin.

Selina solved the problem by producing a couple of pretty muslin dresses that her own children had outgrown.

"They're still quite good and will fit Sawitri perfectly, while allowing her more freedom," she said, "and will repay a little the gratitude I feel for the governor's kindness."

Veena could not suppress a wry smile at the notion of so exalted a child in second-hand clothes. However, they were certainly less restrictive than those she wore, and as Western clothes were not available here, they were a practical solution for the time being. So she took them with thanks and set off back to the palace for lunch, hiring the first samlor she saw.

She had paid off the driver at the palace gates and was making her way around to the back of the building so that she could go directly into her own suite, when she came face to face with Samrit Udom.

She halted, with a surprised "What on earth are you doing

here? If you've been looking for me, you're wasting your time. There can be no friendship between us."

"You flatter yourself, pretty one. You do not make up my entire universe. My business was with another."

Smiling unpleasantly, he passed on.

"I think he came to see Nada," Sawitri piped up. "I have seen him before."

So here was the source of Nada's opium supplies. Veena pursed her lips. The evil trade flourished under the governor's very nose, in spite of his efforts to stamp it out.

She could, of course, inform him of her strong suspicions, but that way might result in the dismissal of Nada, and the enmity of the rest of the palace servants. Her only course, other than ignoring the matter, was to have it out with the old woman herself at the first opportunity.

After their simple lunch of fish curry, pineapple and melon, followed by a short rest, Sawitri demanded to go out into the courtyard to play ball. "In one of my new dresses," she added.

So the pink muslin was donned and the child resembled an unfolding rosebud as she skipped outside in the delightful freedom of bare legs and feet, and shorter, wider skirts.

She had not been playing long, while Veena sat working out a timetable of lessons to be started the following morning, when out came Nada, her wrinkled face dark with disapproval. In an absolute torrent of invective, she made clear her dislike of Sawitri's new attire, and her assertion that the master would not approve.

Before Veena could form an answer, the woman shuffled off to inform the great man himself, for within minutes out he stalked, a distinct frown on his handsome face.

"What is this?" he demanded, in a voice that left no doubt as to how he felt. "I agreed to shared lessons with the English children, but draw the line at dressing my own child in their abbreviated garb. It makes her look like a hoyden showing so much leg. She will be a laughingstock and the talk of the palace!"

Veena flushed painfully. It was devastating to displease him so soon, and humiliating to be rebuked in front of the sly Nada, doubtless lurking within earshot to recount her triumph over her usurper to the rest of the servants.

"I'm sorry to incur your disapproval, my lord," she murmured, "but a long tight pasin is so restrictive to an active child at play. I thought that in the privacy of her courtyard she would have more freedom in Western dress."

"And where, may I ask, in this remote city did you pick up such a garment?"

"The kind English lady gave it to me," Sawitri piped up, hopping around like a bird in her newfound freedom. "It is too small for Vicky and Sally, and now I am like them, I like it."

"What you, or Miss Basche, like is of no consequence in a matter of propriety. You will go and remove it at once and never wear cast-offs again!" Without another word he strode off.

"Must I?" Sawitri said, her lips wobbling.

"I'm afraid so, my dear. We can't disobey a direct order of your father."

But there was now a score to settle with the sly Nada, who flouted him in the matter of opium smoking, yet lost no opportunity to make trouble for one who she considered had deposed her. When the opportunity came, she would have no qualms in settling it, Veena reflected, her blue eyes clouded, because the dark ones of the governor had temporarily lost their brooding tenderness and looked on her with stony disapproval.

It was gone the following morning when, with Vicky, Sally and Sawitri sitting at their small desks, Veena was explaining the alphabet with illustrations on the new blackboard, there came a knock on the door. Without waiting for permission, Taksin Chulasong entered.

He glanced with keen eyes at his small daughter, now demurely clad in long pasin and blouse, and at her two flaxen-haired companions, before saying "Good morning, Miss Basche."

"Good morning, my lord."

"I have here a note from David Lancaster," he went on. "He returned home last night. Tomorrow he goes up-country to inspect some baby elephants and give them a medical examination before passing them fit to start training. When he learned of the arrangement we have come to regarding the children, he was most pleased, and wishes to show his gratitude. He wondered if Sawitri and all of you would like to accompany him on the trip. The camp is not too far off. Just a pleasant morning's sail, along the river and klongs, but it would mean one night's camping. I'm sure Sawitri would love to see the baby elephants, but do you consider she would be all right camping out for the night, Miss Basche?"

Veena's spirits soared. How kind of David to offer to take them. It would be nice to see him again. Generous too of Taksin Chulasong to sweep aside his annoyance of yesterday and consider letting his precious child out of his protection for a couple of days and one night.

"Why, my lord, that's generous of you both!" she said warmly. "I think Sawitri would enjoy the experience immensely and be quite all right sleeping with me."

Sawitri was jumping up and down in great excitement. "Oh, Father, do say that I may go," she begged. "I would love to see the baby elephants."

Her father smiled down on her, and now the austerity was all gone and his face transfigured by loving tenderness. With a shock, Veena realized that she longed with all her heart for him to look at her, too, in just such a manner, but he merely said, "Then pay heed to your lessons this morning and make Miss Basche's task as easy as possible, and you may have the following two days off."

It was not easy to get the full attention of all three children again after he had left, but a threat to cancel the treat if they did not cease their excited chatter finally had them laboriously copying out the alphabet and chanting out what each letter stood for.

Little Sawitri was as intelligent as she was precocious, Veena discovered, and promised to leave the other two behind. Working with such a child would be a joy, and how rewarding to coax the best from her and make her father proud of his one remaining treasure.

CHAPTER NINE

A river trip was the most pleasant of all in this land, avoiding the dust and heat of road travel and revealing the changing riverbank. Scenes of bamboo houses raised on stilts, banana and coconut plantations, ancient temples and dense jungle rioting down to the water's edge.

There was just sufficient room in the longboat for David and his family, together with Veena and Sawitri. They crowded the center of the seatless craft, lounging on rugs in the well, while two Siamese boys navigated the fast flowing Ping River from fore and aft.

They were all in the best of spirits, the three children chattering incessantly, the others delighting in the exhilaration of movement and animation. Laughing brown boys splashing in the shallower water called out to them, passing fishermen waved, and bright-plumaged jungle birds flashed across their path.

"How peaceful and lovely it all is," Selina said to her husband. "I quite envy you if you get many of these trips."

David smiled. "Oh, it isn't all beer and skittles. I get my share of bone-shaking, dusty road travel and the odd brush with a wild animal or cobra. But on the whole I enjoy it all."

He had purposely ordered the boat boys to go quite slowly so that they could all enjoy the scenery. Consequently, their destination was not reached in the expected time. Even the big flat straw hats could not keep the full force of the midday sun off, so when the children complained of being thirsty, he pulled in under the shade of overhanging, slender-trunked betel-nut trees adjoining an open water hole.

"If you keep quiet, you may see an elephant family come down to drink," he said. "There are lots of wild elephants in the vicinity."

Selina and Veena unpacked the picnic basket and doled out fruit drinks, now lukewarm but nonetheless welcome. The boat boys took food and wandered a few yards into the jungle for refreshment and a brief rest, while the rest of them tucked into buttered rolls and hard-boiled eggs, and refreshing segments of pomelo.

Veena had just finished her fruit when David nudged her, a finger to his lips for silence. Following his other pointing finger, her glance encountered a large crocodile climbing sluggishly from the river to settle on the baked mudbank.

"He's hoping to catch some unwary small creature coming down to drink," David whispered. "See his strategic position."

With innate cunning, he had positioned himself behind a tuft of elephant grass which shielded him from the water hole. Here he lay motionless, apparently asleep, but his half-closed eyes very much alert.

Silence had descended on the boat. The three children, repleted and content, lay flat in the carpeted well, hats over their faces. Selina leaned back on the cushion she had brought, eyes closed against the glare. Only Veena and David sat rigidly watching, alert for anything that might happen.

What ugly brutes crocodiles were. No wonder they were feared and hated, she reflected.

There came a stirring from within the jungle and out from the gloom emerged a male elephant, followed by his mate and two offspring.

One looked half grown, but the other was very small, no more than two years old.

The family ambled to the river and began to drink and squirt themselves with water, all except the youngest. He, with youthful bravado, decided to investigate what lay on the other side of the elephant grass.

He stared for a moment at the grey bulk of the crocodile, then with typical baby elephant mischief, began to tease the great creature, prodding the tail with his short trunk in an effort to force it into motion.

David drew in his breath sharply, anticipating disaster. The lifting of the long snout from the mudbank, the opening of the tremendous jaws, the snapping of the cruel teeth around that playful trunk.

Veena, her eyes glued to the impending drama, sensed him drawing his gun from its holster in defense of the elephant. He did not need to use it. The mother, with an uncanny sense of danger, ceased her drinking, moved swiftly around the patch of elephant grass, threw her trunk around her wayward offspring and dragged him away, just in time.

"Phew, that was a narrow shave for the youngster," David gasped, "but I guess he'll be more careful in future. His mother's doing her best to teach him the error of his ways."

Veena laughed at the sight of the mother, back at the waterhole, spanking the youngster soundly with her trunk. The disturbance roused the children, who sat up and watched with delight while the crocodile slid back into the water to await some easier prey and the elephants resumed their water activities.

"They're almost as intelligent as humans and more lovable," Veena said. "No wonder your work brings so much satisfaction, David."

"True, and it's time we were off." He whistled for the boat boys, Selina stowed the picnic remains in the basket, and then they were off on the last short lap of the journey down a canal that turned off from the river.

They soon reached the great clearing where the elephant nursery was situated. Here lived about a dozen mother beasts with their young, until the offspring were passed strong and fit enough to leave the sanctuary and join the training center at around three years old.

The children were in their element at seeing so many little jumbos together. They watched the playful antics with shrieks of laughter, fed them bananas and other dainties, got themselves squirted with water and plastered with mud and had a great deal of fun.

Meanwhile David gave each youngster a thorough examination in turn. He seemed well pleased with them and passed all as healthy except one. This one needed extra food and care. He gave the necessary instructions to its keeper, then picked out four robust three-year-olds to be sent to the training school.

The afternoon was now far spent. It would soon be dark.

"We'll erect the tents and then have a meal," he said. "I've brought two small ones along, preferring them to being eaten alive by bugs inside the sleeping huts."

The boys soon had them up, then served a meal of rice, vegetables and fish. Simple but tasty. By now the children were almost asleep on their feet. They were put to bed and the adults were soon glad to follow them.

Lying awake in the tiny enclosure by the edge of the clearing, with Sawitri breathing evenly beside her, Veena listened to the night noises of the forest. Mysterious rustlings, harsh calls and the occasional deeper note of some larger animal on the prowl mingled with the croaking of frogs, but she was not afraid. A stout fence of bamboo enclosed the whole of the camp, keeping out intruders. She fell asleep thinking of Taksin Chulasong, back in his luxurious palace. Did he miss the child? Was he anxious about her? There was surely no need.

Yet in spite of all she awakened sometime later with a start and a strong foreboding that something was amiss. It was very dark inside the tent, and absolutely silent, without the faintest sound of stirring or breathing from Sawitri. Anxiously, she groped on the pallet beside her where the child should have been and found nothing.

Fear caught at her throat, almost choking her. Desperately, she sprang to her feet and, without waiting to pull anything on over her cotton nightdress, pulled aside the tent flap and dashed outside.

Here the moon shed some light. By its aid she detected a movement down by the river, where one of the elephants had knocked down a section of the fence, leaving a way through. A dark figure sprinted through the opening, and from the same direction came a stifled little cry that was almost certainly the child's voice.

Sawitri was being kidnaped.

Imagining Taksin Chulasong's grief and rage if anything should happen to her, Veena gave vent to a piercing scream, calculated to wake the dead, followed by another. They had instant effect. Within seconds, from David's tent close by, he came running, gun in hand, clad only in shorts.

"What's wrong?" he demanded.

"Someone's taken Sawitri. I've just seen them disappearing through that gap in the fence." She pointed with shaking finger.

"Damnation! You go in with Selina. I'll go after them. Whoever it is, is bound to keep to the river track. The jungle's too dense to penetrate just there."

He had already started in pursuit as he spoke. What a blessing he invariably slept with his gun by his side while up-country, she reflected. Also he was so splendidly fit that he could outrun most of the natives. He would soon catch up with his quarry.

All the same, she was shaking like a leaf when she crept into the family tent to find Selina sitting up on her pallet, white-faced and obviously terrified. The two children, exhausted by the long day, still slept peacefully alongside.

"Sawitri has been kidnaped," Veena whispered. "Fortunately, I sensed something was happening and woke up. When I dashed outside, I just caught a glimpse of the villain disappearing through a gap in the fence down by the river."

"How awful!" Selina grasped her hand and pulled her down beside her. "You must be in torment, but don't despair, my dear. If David's only a few yards behind, he's bound to catch up with a Siamese burdened with a child. His gun will help a lot. He can shoot to wound or even over the kidnaper's head if he's afraid of hitting Sawitri. David's awfully cool-headed in an emergency. He's had too many close shaves not to be ready for anything when up-country."

Comforted slightly, Veena sat clasping Selina's hand, but all she could think of was Taksin. She had betrayed his trust in her, she felt, and if David's pursuit was not a hundred percent successful, her own fate, and his too, could be anything from instant dismissal to imprisonment or even death. A governor in this remote northern province was all-powerful.

But even transcending her fear for her own and David's punishment should anything happen to the child was her terrible anxiety on Taksin's behalf. After the cruel blows already hurled at him by fate, the thought of his one remaining comfort being torn from him was too poignant to be borne. Life would become intolerable for him.

The next ten minutes dragged by with nerve-wracking slowness. There was not even the slight relief of action. All she could do was crouch there, clutching Selina's hand and praying for some sound that would mean David's return.

It came at last. His bare feet were noiseless on the hard beaten ground, but the sound of his voice reassuring the little girl brought a surge of thankfulness to both the women. Before either of them could make a move, the tent flap was pulled aside and he entered, Sawitri clinging to his neck.

"She's all right, thank God." He thrust the small bundle into Veena's arms and mopped his damp forehead.

At first Veena could find no words, then hugging her charge closely, she managed. "I can never thank you enough. Did you have any trouble?"

"Not really. Whoever it was could darn well run, though! Eventually I had to fire at his legs to stop him before he left the path and I lost him. I must have hit him, for he dropped the child and fled with a yell. By the time I'd picked her up, he was out of sight. He must be wounded, if not seriously."

For the remainder of the night Veena stayed where she was, while David occupied the other tent, sitting on guard with the flap open in case there were any further incidents. However, all was quiet and she even managed to doze off at last, Sawitri still clasped in her arms.

It seemed like a bad dream the following morning. David questioned the elephant boys, but none of them had heard or seen anything, nor could they shed any light on the incident.

"I'll stake my life on their loyalty," he said. "Whoever was responsible has no direct connection with the camp, and yet it must have been someone who knew the governor's child would be here overnight. Could it be some villain who has a grudge against you, or even me, trying to bring down the great man's wrath on us and so get us thrown out, I wonder? Who at the palace knew where you and Sawitri were going?"

Veena suddenly saw the light. "There's one person who bears me no love. The child's old nurse. She considers I've supplanted her and detests all the innovations I've brought with me. She'd surely never harm her old charge though, and how could her influence reach all this way off?"

David reflected. "Maybe she has some contact who could do the dirty work for her and hide the child safely until you'd been suitably punished and banished."

Again Veena had a flash of inspiration. "Samrit Udom, of course!" she burst out. "He supplies her with drugs and has few scruples. He hates me for spurning his advances and, come to think of it, hates you even more for being given the post he covets himself. He even bears enmity toward the governor, too, because he's trying to stamp out the growing of opium poppies and drug trafficking. It's no secret that Udom's father encourages the hill tribes to defy the regulations and takes most of the profit, but he's too sly to be caught."

"I've heard of him," David said, "and the remote hill tribes openly smoke their opium pipes. They disguise their growing plots so cunningly, though, and change their location so frequently that it would take a really determined search to find them, and that would be dangerous. They'd never let you get away to tell the tale."

Even in the morning sunlight, Veena shivered. "It seems clear who instigated the outrage, but of course he'd pay some thug to do his dirty work and take care not to be directly involved. From now on we must both be very careful, David. You in particular are vulnerable, traveling around your remote districts."

"I'm always on the alert. Don't worry about me, my dear."

Soon after breakfast Selina, Veena and the children set off for the return river journey, while David sailed farther upriver to one of the lumber camps where teak was sawed into logs, formed into

great rafts and started off on their long, floating journey toward
Bangkok. All with the indispensable help of the willing, powerful
elephants.

Veena was too preoccupied to really enjoy it. The thought of
telling Taksin of the incident weighed heavily. There was no question of trying to deceive him. Sawitri would certainly make the
most of her unpleasant adventure. Veena tried to picture his reaction at what could have been a much more serious eventuality, but
it was beyond her. She only knew that if he dismissed her it would
be a wounding blow that would take some getting over. If ever she
did.

They reached the palace around midday, just as the sun was
becoming uncomfortably hot. Taksin Chulasong came immediately to their suite to welcome his daughter and ask how she had
enjoyed her trip. Fortunately, she was so full of the charm and
sagacity of the elephants that she omitted any mention of her
night experience, and Nada appeared to whisk the child away to
wash off the dust before she could recall it.

"So the trip was a success and Sawitri looks happier and more
animated than she has done for some time," Taksin said, smiling
down on Veena. Even in this moment of truth, when she was
about to incur his possible anger, she felt herself thrilling to his
magnetism. As tall and virile as David, with that touch of haunt-
ing sadness in his eyes that gave his handsome features an added
attraction. A man who ached for the love he had lost. A man to
love, if he could only bring himself to love another woman.

But she was treading dangerous ground, she reminded herself
sharply. A commoner and a palace servant, even on the top level,
it was presumptuous indeed to look on him with anything save
respect and awe. With his distant royal connections and commanding position, a gulf lay between them that nothing could
bridge.

"What troubles you?" he demanded. "I detect a conflict in your
face."

"Why, something that occurred during the night," she said,
brushing aside anything else. She went on to relate the nerve-
wracking incident, ending, "We have David Lancaster to thank

for rescuing her so promptly, before any harm could befall her. If anyone is to be punished, please let it be me, as he certainly doesn't deserve it."

He stood for a moment, lips taut, then said slowly:

"In fairness, neither do you, Miss Basche. I confess had my child not returned, or been injured in any way, my pain and grief could have blinded me to justice and I might have punished you both. As things are, the incident apparently made so little impression on her that she even forgot to mention it. Some bandit from the hill country possibly found out Sawitri's identity and tried to kidnap her for ransom. There are too many mixed and half-wild tribes in the hills bordering Burma, and the Shans, particularly, are growing insubordinate. If they don't mend their ways, I may be forced to send an expedition to shake them up, and destroy any poppy-growing areas we can find."

Veena sighed. So much for her hopes of helping the women with a small traveling clinic.

"What is this? You surely do not side with them?" he said, and now his frown was quite fierce.

"Not really. I was only thinking of the women and children, my lord. I had hopes of eventually going among them to help and teach them and cut down the infant mortality rate."

"A pipe dream!" he said roughly. "It would be too dangerous for you. Even the missionaries have had no success with the more remote tribes, and now leave them severely alone, for their own safety."

She was silent, not knowing what to say. At last he broke in. "If it is any consolation, Miss Basche, I will tell you an ambition of mine. I hope to found a fine new university and hospital on the outskirts of the city, in memory of my late wife and children. It will be open to anyone in need, and you shall be one of the first to start work there, for Sawitri will only need you for a couple of years."

She murmured her thanks, still somehow vaguely disappointed, scarcely comprehending his next words.

"I am glad you have the child in your charge, for in a few days the palace will be a hive of activity and I shall not be able to give her much attention. The King, my cousin several times removed, in whose hands we all are, from the highest to the lowest in the land, has intimated that it is high time I married again and begat a son. Without a son to follow him, a ruler or a governor is in a most vulnerable position, open to intrigue and all sorts of trouble, he points out. Consequently, he is sending Prince Roma, another distant relative, and his daughter Princess Duangta, to visit for a week, and hopes this will end in a betrothal. Whatever my own feelings, I am bound to entertain them and their servants, though I confess the prospect is not to my taste. I fear I have selfishly sunk too deeply in my own grief. Perhaps for Sawitri's sake I should have married again, and given her a more normal life."

It was certainly unusual, Veena reflected, for a virile man of around thirty-five to remain aloof to women for so long. Many of his contemporaries kept a harem of several wives. And, without doubt, it would be better for Sawitri to be part of a real family again. Yet an absurd and unreasoning jealousy of this Princess Duangta consumed her, in spite of everything.

Although lessons with the Lancaster children went on as usual for the next few days, the air of excitement and anticipation pervading the palace penetrated even to the seclusion of their small rear suite. The servants scurried around, sweeping, dusting and renovating the ornate front rooms, brightening them with flowering shrubs and sweet-smelling frangipani and preparing a mountain of food.

Prince Roma was bringing a most impressive gift for the man he hoped would soon become his son-in-law. This was a near-white young albino elephant that had recently been captured in a remote jungle. Such a beast, as Veena well knew, was thought to be a reincarnation of the Buddha by the superstitious Siamese, and revered accordingly. It should bring good fortune to Taksin Chulasong, the palace in general and the entire city. As was the custom, it would be installed in the elephant kraol with due ceremony, given a name, and live the rest of its life in pampered luxury.

When the afternoon for the arrival of the prince and his daughter came, Sawitri was all impatience to see the young princess who might soon be her new mother. Having no recollection of her own mother, this was natural enough, Veena conceded, while trying to curb the child's impetuosity.

"You must not intrude on the important arrival but must wait until you're sent for after dinner," she said firmly, "but knowing how eager for a glimpse you are, we'll contrive a hiding place where you can watch unnoticed." She would not admit to herself that she was just as eager as Sawitri to see this princess who might in due course be installed here as mistress of the domestic side.

She was bound to take to the child, Veena reflected, so sweet and small in her brand-new tunic and pasin of deep pink, embroidered with seed pearls. Together they found a nook in the impressive outer hall, screened by a mass of exotic scented frangipani in a great Chinese vase. How beautiful it was, with its waxy flowers of white, cream and rosy pink in great clusters. The life tree, as it was universally known. The flower of immortality. It grew profusely around the temples and lived forever, it was said.

Sawitri squatted down on the rush matting, legs crossed before her like a small Buddha, while Veena settled on a padded stool. They had not long to wait before there was a flurry of servants to the open door, and after them strode Taksin Chulasong to greet his guests.

Veena's pulse quickened at the sight of him, magnificent in richly embroidered tunic and long satin trousers in place of the shorter baggy pants he sometimes wore. Now he looked every inch a prince, even though he was not entitled to the term. Surely it must have been his training in many sports that had given him such a physique, so superior to his fellow Siamese. This princess could not possibly fail to fall in love with him, but would he fall for her? What would she be like?

A few moments later Veena saw for herself. Following her father came a small, slight figure in a jade green pasin and cream tunic encrusted with jewels that flashed and glowed in a slanting beam of sunlight. But the most striking thing about her was her extreme youth. She could not be more than sixteen.

Her small face was as smooth and round as Sawitri's, utterly devoid of experience. At twenty-three, Veena, with life in the raw as she had lived it in the clinic, with all the maladies of the poor confronting her, felt an absolute veteran beside this sheltered child.

"She looks pretty," Sawitri whispered. "I think I shall like her."

Veena scarcely heard. How could such naïve innocence satisfy a man like Taksin Chulasong in either intellect or body, after the legendary wife he had lost?

She was still trying to quell the tumult within her of shock, jealousy and doubt when the visitors had passed with their host into the next apartment, and she and Sawitri were able to leave their hiding place and return to the nursery suite.

Sawitri chattered like a magpie. She at least approved of this pretty visitor who seemed almost as much a child as herself.

CHAPTER TEN

The following day had been declared a public holiday in honor of the elephant. Installing a new white elephant was a rare and important occasion. The rites could only be performed by a person of high rank with some royal blood, and were welcomed with great enthusiasm by the citizens of Chiengmai as a highlight in their humdrum lives.

In the late afternoon the striking-looking beast was brought to the enclosure in front of the palace, followed by as many of the common people as could crowd in. Beside the palace entrance a platform had been erected, complete with several rows of seats. Here, Taksin Chulasong, his guests and important members of the city took their places, with little Sawitri at the feet of Princess Duangta. The princess, who appeared to have taken a liking to the child, had expressed a desire that she might watch the ceremony too, a desire enthusiastically granted by the child's father.

Veena, feeling left out and unwanted, was forced to be content to peep from behind the erection in the company of the perfidious Nada, hiding her chagrin as best she could.

The rites were performed with due ceremony by Taksin. Gravely he lighted candles and joss sticks, and presented new orange robes to the priests. Then the elephant was anointed with sweet oil, and he was officially named Phra Sawet Phalongson. Afterward, the great victory drum was beaten, and music broke out on all sides from gamelan orchestras outside and inside the enclosure. There was feasting and a display of classical dancing by

pretty girls in gorgeous costumes and with fearsome artificial
nails.

Not one of them outshone demure Princess Duangta, her lovely
black hair adorned with pink frangipani to match her dress.

"She will make a fitting mother for Sawitri," Nada declared
with satisfaction. "It is high time the governor wed again."

Veena could stand no more. Already she felt quite superfluous.
With pain searing her heart, she slipped out into the streets, noisy
and gay with flags and bunting, clashing cymbals, striking gongs
and beating drums.

Without conscious thought, she found herself walking in the
direction of the clinic. If and when Taksin married, she was thinking, she would return there. It would be too galling to stay on at
the palace with these turbulent emotions tormenting her. Emotions which she had no right to feel.

It was only when she found herself outside the clinic that she
realized it would probably be closed. On a public holiday the staff
would not turn up for work, nor would any patients.

Yet on trying the door she found it open, and there in his office
was Father Joseph, working under his hanging oil lamp.

"You are one of the few working today," she chided. "Why are
you not out enjoying yourself?"

He smiled gently. "Crowds and noise are not my idea of fun,
Veena, and there is always work to be done here. More to the
point, why are *you* not enjoying yourself at the palace, for that,
after all, is the focal point of the gaity."

She shrugged. "I seem to be quite superfluous today. The visiting princess has taken Sawitri under her wing so she has no need
of me."

"So the talk of the governor marrying again is no idle gossip.
Well, I hope it works out for him. He has been alone long enough.
Also he is a good friend to me and my work."

He took off his spectacles and mopped his brow and eyes.

"You look all in, Father. I believe you've been here for most of
the day. Surely you can finish now and go home. What's so urgent?"

"The anopheles mosquito, my child. There's a plague of them

in some of the hill villages this year. The Pao tribe are particularly hard hit with malaria and I hear the death rate is high, especially among the children. I'm getting together supplies of drugs like quinine and other aids, also special foods for the small ones. I intend to send help next week. Father John has volunteered to go. You recall him? He did most of his training here and is now qualified for basic treatments."

Veena remembered the bony redhead, earnest and hard-working. "What help will he have?" she asked.

"Woefully little. Chesda will go as bodyguard, to cook his food and give what assistance he can. If only we had a spare nurse to attend the women and children, I should be happier. They might refuse ministration by a man, yet we have no one we can send at the moment."

She was suddenly all attention. Here was work crying out to be done. Work that she was trained for and had originally hoped to do. It seemed criminal to be dallying at the palace with one small child who would soon have little need of her.

"I'll gladly volunteer if the governor will release me," she said breathlessly.

His face lit up. "That would be marvelous. You're just about the best and most sensible girl I ever trained, but you must tread warily. We can't afford to offend one of our friends, and so powerful too."

It was agreed that she should mention the project to Taksin Chulasong at the first opportunity. With the palace in turmoil, this might be difficult, but fortunately the visitors would not be staying long.

"It will be several days before our arrangements are complete and Father John is ready to start off," Father Joseph said. "You know how slow they are to move in this land, and how nothing can be rushed. So see what you can do. I should like to get the work over and as many as possible treated before the monsoon begins. River travel can be hazardous then, with mountain torrents and floods."

She promised to report back as soon as possible and left him, feeling less despondent than when she had arrived.

No opportunity to speak privately to Taksin presented itself during the next two days. He did not come to the schoolroom in the mornings. His entire day seemed to be occupied with the entertainment of his guests. But on the following morning, as Veena and the children were taking a break in their private courtyard, she was surprised to see him emerge from the open door.

Her heart jolted within her. She had to steel herself to remain impassive as he began to stroll around beside her.

"Already you have worked wonders with Sawitri, Miss Basche," he said, glancing with satisfaction at the child as she hopped and skipped around the fountain with her two small companions. "She is so much more lively and ready for anything. The princess is already fond of her and wishes to take the child back to her home for a short visit. My guests will be leaving tomorrow. Do you consider it would be good for Sawitri to go?"

Veena stared, scarcely knowing what to answer. Surely she would not be required to go too.

At last she said stiffly. "Why yes, my lord, I think she is ready to go off on her own for a while. The experience will help to prepare her for school later on."

He nodded. "Precisely my own views. And the arrangement fits in quite well with my own plans, as I shall be going to the capital on business."

"To Bangkok, my lord?" She could not conceal her surprise.

"I need to see the King about certain formalities regarding my future marriage." His tone was abrupt and harsh, as though the words were dragged unwillingly from him.

Her hands clenched so that the nails bit into the soft palms. "I wish you happiness, lord," she said at last.

He stopped violently in his tracks. "Spare me such conventional felicitations, if you please. You, of all people, have no need of such shams. It will be a marriage of convenience, nothing more. A bowing to pressure. From the King down to the meanest of my people here in Chiengmai. Plus the need to give my daughter a mother, and myself an heir to avoid discord later on. Maybe even war."

Emotion warred within her. Sorrow that his first love still

blinded him to the lure of all other women, barring him from fulfillment; unworthy gladness that the little doll of a princess had not yet captured his heart.

"Perhaps in time, my lord," she began. He cut her short.

"She is a child! As immature and naïve as Sawitri herself. Why could she not have been someone like you?"

His mutinous gaze fastened on her night black hair, her blue eyes and honey-cream skin, and slid slowly downward over voluptuous breasts under filmy blouse, and the curving hips revealed by the clinging pasin.

What was he saying? The world around her fell away in one blinding flash. This was almost a confession that he felt the same way about her as she felt about him, brief as was their acquaintance. In silence they confronted one another.

The scent of the frangipani by the fountain stole out with unbearable sweetness. The flower of immortality, that bloomed for Lord Buddha and for lovers. It mocked her with glimpses of Nirvana that could never be fulfilled, because the gap between them was a yawning chasm. She was a commoner, with far back a trace of British ancestry that showed in her blue eyes. He was of the royal house, however far removed, and must marry to please the King and the people of this northern province he governed.

"Dangerous talk, my lord. The palace has ears and eyes," she murmured, thinking of Nada and her sly eavesdropping.

With a violent gesture, he began to walk on again. Veena, her emotions too chaotic to think clearly, remembered Father Joseph and his need of her. It seemed like a lifeline to keep her afloat.

"With Sawitri away for a while, I shall not be needed here, my lord," she began. "I saw Father Joseph yesterday. He is in desperate need of nursing help for a short time. I should be grateful if you would release me to do what he trained me for."

Taksin considered. "That seems fair and just," he conceded at last. "It would be wrong of me to insist on your wasting your time here. But only for three weeks at most. Then you must promise to come back to Sawitri, and to me."

She tried to ignore the last three words. This mission to the hills should be over by then. Father Joseph was anxious to complete it before the monsoon broke. Caution prompted her to conceal the venture from Taksin Chulasong. He would surely forbid it, considering there could be hazards. Let him believe that she would be working at the clinic only.

"I promise, lord."

"Then you may go tomorrow as soon as Sawitri leaves. I myself shall be leaving at the same time for the river trip to Bangkok."

A long journey but a pleasant one, floating rapidly with the current in his spacious private barge, with living and sleeping quarters and the small canopied deck where he could sit and watch the passing river traffic and the banks, full of human interest. So different from her own trip upriver, in a smaller more austere boat, with few pretensions at comfort. Venturing into the wild and primitive hill country.

The children came skipping over. Intimate conversation was at an end. Taksin glanced at her for a long moment with an expression that said what words could not, then turned and went inside.

Without the touch that she craved, yet knew was too dangerous. Just to feel his fingers twining about her own, his hand caressing her cheek, his lips touching hers was an ecstasy she could never hope to know, and the knowledge was a bitter pill within her.

Father Joseph was overjoyed when she walked into the clinic the following day with the news that she had three weeks' leave.

"Splendid! Now you and Father John can get together and discuss plans. He wants to set out at dawn tomorrow."

Over a cup of coffee in the small rest room, she and the gangling, redheaded young priest pored over a rough sketch of the Toa country.

"The malaria outbreak is centered in the Toa village," he said, "so that is where we'll set up our temporary clinic. When we've dealt with the villagers there, we can make forays into the surrounding country. Anywhere that seems to need aid, and we can reach by a short river trip."

Malaria was endemic here in northern Siam. A certain control could be kept in Chiengmai, with liberal doses of quinine and regular cleaning of the klongs, but out in the hill country it was a different matter. From time to time there would be an explosion in the number of anopheles strain of mosquitos, breeding in stagnant pools, and the steady rate of malaria would rise—and so would the resultant death toll. Until recently, no one had cared or been able to help, but now Father Joseph felt impelled to contact these people if they would not or could not contact him.

Their resources were meager, Veena realized, the main one being a plentiful supply of quinine. They would also take powerful disinfectant to treat any stagnant water not used by the tribes and so help to kill off larvae. Father John had a smattering of medical knowledge and practice, as she herself had. No doubt they would be called on to use it in various ways if the native witch doctor's magic had failed.

"I put a lot of faith in natural herbal remedies," Father John said. "I'm hoping to gather a store of eucalyptus leaves to bring back to the clinic, also some chaulmoogra nuts. The oil distilled from them has a beneficial effect on leprosy, I've found."

Veena found herself warming to him. His dedication was patent and together they should be able to accomplish something worthwhile in the short time available to them.

As soon as the afternoon heat had waned, she walked briskly to the Lancaster bungalow to tell Selina of the venture and that she would not be able to have the children for the next three weeks.

"Maybe not after that," she said. "The governor is to be married soon, and I can't say whether I'll be needed then, or want to stay on. The clinic is very short of skilled help."

"I'm not too keen on the idea of your going among the hill tribes," David, who happened to be at home, said. "On the face of it they're harmless, but withdrawn and reserved. You might get scant cooperation or thanks if you try to penetrate too deeply. They're spirit worshipers you know, and prefer their witch doctor to foreigners' medicine."

"But in this instance his remedies seem to be useless," Veena pointed out. "They'll surely accept ours in desperation. Father John has traveled briefly among them and can make himself understood, he tells me."

The hill people were not true Siamese but chiefly of Chinese descent, with their own customs, language and dress. Relations between them and the Siamese were not cordial, but they usually kept themselves aloof and caused no trouble. Only now, when the government in Bangkok was trying to stamp out the opium poppy and its nefarious trade, was there a threat of strain in the situation.

"Father John will have his gun, of course, to procure fresh meat. In the last resort he could use it in defense, but we're not expecting anything so drastic as that," Veena said.

"All the same, I'll be glad when you're safely back in Chiengmai," David said. "Incidentally, I'll be visiting my most northern lumber camp soon, at the junction of the Ping River and the Licok. I'll try to make time to contact you at the Pao village. That's where you'll be stationed, I guess, since the outbreak seems worst there."

She nodded. "It will be nice if you can. I wish I could speak their language, but I suppose I'll manage with a little help from Father John."

The pale mist still hung over the river when she, Father John and their boatman Chesda set out the following morning. Chesda sat in the stern, working with his long punting pole, while Veena and Father John lounged in the prow. In between, the well of the boat was piled solid with medical supplies, food and other necessities.

"It's hard going, punting against the current," Father John said, "but if I take turns with Chesda, we'll make it before nightfall. Fortunately, the river is low and sluggish. During the monsoon, we'd never make it so far upriver."

Veena thought of Taksin, floating with the current the opposite way in his luxurious private barge. It had been hard to see him go, with the public gaze upon him and no chance of a private word of farewell. Sawitri had left happily enough, seated beside the princess in a little open carriage drawn by a mule, while the rest of their retinue rode muleback to their own palace.

The riverside scenery grew wilder the farther up-country they penetrated. Now there were few houses on stilts, and little river traffic. An occasional fishing boat passed, or a few boys could be seen bathing near the riverbank. Impenetrable jungle pressed close on either side for some of the way, and beyond it rose high and rugged hills.

Toward midday they drew up by a bare, stony spit of land, climbed from the boat and stretched their cramped limbs. Chesda laid out a simple meal, and after they had eaten they rested for an hour in the shade of a great banyan tree.

"Time to push off again," Father John said rising, "if we are to reach there well before nightfall and fix the tent."

They had not been traveling for long when they reached the lumber camp mentioned by David the day before. Great teak logs, sawed into uniform lengths, lay around in piles in an open clearing, waiting for the monsoon to swell the waters. Then they would be lashed together into huge rafts, pushed into the river by elephants and floated downriver toward the far coast. One of the boys would actually make his home on each of these moving platforms, living on it for the weeks it would take to negotiate the long trail to Bangkok. Keeping it on the move and making sure it was not pirated by rogues. Teak was a readily saleable commodity and brought many bahts to Siam, hence the importance of David's position, and the bitter enmity of Samrit Udom, who coveted it for himself.

There were no elephants to be seen. They did little work during this hot dry season, and would be roaming the jungle in the vicinity of the camp, foraging their own food. Once tamed, they never strayed far away, and were rounded up by their mahouts whenever they were needed.

Chesda steered the boat into the side river branching off into the jungle. Now they were in a twilight atmosphere, sultry and steamy beneath the overhanging trees that almost met above them. Strange calls sounded from the crowding trees, bright birds flashed across their path, monkeys chattered and peered at them and insects plagued them. Perspiration drenched them, streaming into their eyes and tasting salt on their lips.

Presently the hills rose high on either side. The jungle thinned until it was a mere strip along the river. Elsewhere, trees and bushes clothed the hillside but with less density.

"We are nearing the Pao village," Father John said. "To reach it, we have to leave the boat and climb about a quarter of a mile up into the hills. Watch out for an open landing place on the right."

"What about our stores?" Veena said.

"What we can't carry on our backs can be brought up later. Ah, here's where we take the trail."

A baked-mud clearing opened before them, with several boats moored alongside a rough landing jetty of teak and bamboo. They eased their boat in, tied it up and each fixed a bundle of the stores to his back.

It was a hard climb, and soon they were all panting and sweating, even though the sun was now low in the sky and there was a hint of mountain coolness in the air.

"Why can't they build their villages on the riverbanks as the Siamese do?" Veena wondered.

"They feel safer hidden away up among the trees and undergrowth," Chesda explained. "Remember, they were originally aliens."

The village appeared quite suddenly. A haphazard collection of ramshackle huts constructed of bamboo poles, rough bits of teak and thatched roofs of palm leaves sweeping almost to the ground. Split bamboo water conduits passed among them, held high on poles, carrying water from hill springs and streams. Thin, dirty pigs foraged among the low scrub bushes between the huts, and scrawny hens scratched at the dusty earth.

"I don't see any cultivated land," Veena said, wiping the sweat from her eyes with the back of her hand.

"Oh, there will be some close by," Father John said. "Rice is their staple food, helped out by fish, pig and poultry meat, pumpkins and chilis."

Roused perhaps by the strange voices, half-clothed children sprang into view from the concealing scrub, along with several women. The women had Chinese-Burmese faces, plump and round, with slanting almond eyes. They stopped dead when they saw the white-skinned Father John, then broke into an excited babble which Veena could not understand.

Father John held up his hand in a gesture of friendship and said a few halting words. They seemed to reassure the women, who edged a little closer.

Their dress was not unattractive. Rough homespun skirts dyed bright red with vegetable dyes, toppled by a loose tunic of the same stuff. The tunics were richly embroidered with colored stitching and beads, and many silver bracelets encircled their brown arms. All had turbanlike headdresses and bare feet.

Now a couple of men appeared, more soberly clad and with pigtails hanging down their backs. Father John made another halting speech and they went off to fetch the *toom sai Kong.*

"That will be the witch doctor, who virtually rules the village," Father John explained. "But don't worry, he's not an alarming savage in weird dress and mask. He just happens to be skilled in spirit lore and strange healing rites, and looks much like the other men."

This individual soon materialized, followed by more of the village folk. Father John told him they had come to help with the malaria problem and any other sicknesses that were proving too difficult for him to handle.

At first he seemed suspicious and uncooperative, but presently admitted that many of the villagers were suffering and too many had died, and so he would accept their help. When asked for accommodation, he pointed out a ramshackle hut that seemed on the point of collapse.

"We'll have to make the best of it for our brief stay." Father John led the way and thankfully they set down their burdens.

The cupboardlike apartment enclosed by bamboo was just big enough to sleep the two men, while the open verandah would hold their stores and form the clinic. By now it was growing dark and they set up the tent alongside. Veena was glad that she would sleep in it, free from the insects of the huts.

"We'll bring up the other supplies tomorrow," Father John said. "At the moment we need rest and sleep."

The next few days proved both busy and interesting for Veena. She and Father John doled out quinine and other remedies to all who came for them, plus vaccinations against smallpox and such tropical scourges. The more seriously ill were visited in their huts, and then they made short forays to other villages.

Veena took to the women, even though they could communicate only by signs. Most of them smoked opium in rough wooden pipes, but they were kind in their crude way, welcomed her into their mean little huts and pressed gifts of embroidered caps, fruit and anything else they had upon her.

By the end of a fortnight their task seemed completed, and they were ready to start back. Then Father John, scrambling down a steep hill-side from a last visit he had made to an outlying hut where an old man lay dying, stumbled on a loose stone and sprained his ankle. By the time he had managed to limp down to the village, the ankle was extremely painful and swollen to twice its size.

"A bad sprain," Veena said, bandaging it with a cold compress. "You'll be forced to rest it up for a day or two. We'll just have to wait until you're fit to travel."

So when an urgent message came that a child was having difficulty in breathing and his mother feared that he would choke, Veena, of course, prepared to set out with the woman who had brought the message.

"Chesda had better go along with you. I don't recall seeing this woman before. She probably comes from an outlying hut and you might not easily find your way back, especially if it's growing dark," Father John said.

Veena shook her head. "I'll do better on my own. The women and children are shy of strange men. If I don't finish until late, I'll stay the night and return tomorrow. Chesda can take care of you."

She slung a canvas bag containing various instruments and medicines over her shoulder and set off with the woman.

The village was soon left behind. They pushed on through scrub and trees, climbing all the time. Veena could not make out any visible track, but the woman seemed sure of her way.

Vague unease assailed her. She had not bargained on going so far out in the wilds on her own, yet it was pointless to remonstrate. Without Father John, she could only communicate with these people by signs.

At last, to her great relief, they came upon a small village. The woman led her to one of the huts, called out a few words to the occupants and vanished.

It was only a little better than the one used by Father John. The sleeping enclosure was bigger, but held only a couple of straw pallets, several stools and some rough shelves for clothes. The floor was covered with rice straw, and on this by one of the pallets knelt a young woman.

The child lying there was obviously hers, and just as obviously in a precarious state. As bad a case of croup as Veena had ever seen. Each breath was a rasping, gasping agony, alternating with a hard cough. Too late for soothing syrups or any other palliative now. Without intervention, the victim would never survive the night.

A tremor of dismay shot through her at the ordeal before her. The thought of cutting into that small throat and inserting a tube in this primitive hut full of germs was daunting in the extreme. Even in the sterile safety of the clinic, with various medical aids, she had never done it herself, though she had aided Father Joseph with the operation on several occasions. How she longed for him now, or even Father John.

With neither available and no time to lose, she must do the best she could, although the penalty, if her efforts failed, might well be her own death.

A fire of wood chippings smoldered among stones on the open verandah, as was the custom among these hill tribes. All cooking was done on it, and in the chilly hill winters it was a focal point around which the family would crouch for warmth. Veena extracted the small scalpel from her canvas bag, together with a tiny throat tube, and hastened out to the fire.

A cauldron of steaming water was slung above it. Taking a clean gourd from a shelf, she dipped it in the water, then put in her instruments to sterilize.

The mother had followed her and stood peering fearfully at her. If only they could communicate, it would be a relief for them both. Veena tried to induce her to remain on the verandah, not knowing how she would react to the business of the knife, but in vain. The woman trailed after her into the sleeping cubicle and crouched down, waiting with expressionless face.

Veena extracted the flask of chloroform from her canvas bag, sprinkled a few drops on a piece of gauze and held it to the laboring nostrils and mouth of the child. Almost immediately he slumped into a state of unconsciousness.

Wishing there were more light, she took up the scalpel and quickly, before her nerve failed or the mother could make some protesting movement that would distract her attention and prove fatal, she made the required cut in the child's throat. Then with a swift, deft movement, she inserted the tube and closed the skin flap over it.

Two or three stitches would keep the wound closed. With some difficulty, she made the required suture, liberally added antiseptic, and bound a piece of sterile gauze around the neck, just as the child began to stir.

And now, miraculously, he was breathing more normally. The terrible rasping sound was gone, the blueness was fading from the lips, the pinched nostrils had relaxed.

Veena motioned the mother to come forward just as her little boy opened his eyes and smiled weakly. Instantly the mother was all smiles. She patted Veena on the back and gave every sign she could of her pleasure.

Now the reaction set in for Veena. She felt as limp as a piece of her own gauze in the confined space, with the sickly smell of chloroform hanging around. She had better get outside before she fainted or made some such exhibition of herself.

She put away her medical kit, then, pointing to her bag, tried to make the woman understand by signs that she would be coming back. She would be obliged to spend the night here to keep her eye on the child, and then tomorrow she would perhaps be able to remove the tube.

The woman seemed to comprehend and smiled as Veena left the hut to breathe in great gulps of fresh air. But she wanted to leave the squalid little village behind for a while. There was time for a brief walk before the light faded, and a faint track led further up into the hills. She would follow it a little way and so restore her equilibrium.

So she set off, climbing slowly between the bushes and trees in the hush of late afternoon before the night creatures came out to break the silence.

How surprised and pleased Father Joseph would be, she was thinking, when she returned to Chiengmai and told him of her first operation entirely on her own. This was good and worthwhile work, helping these remote people, as she had always hoped to do, before Taksin Chulasong burst upon her world with an impact more profound than any she had known before. But it was only a pipe dream, and a dangerous one at that. Soon he would be married, and then on one pretext or another she would be forced to leave the palace, for to stay there would be both difficult and hazardous. Sawitri was already friends with the little doll princess and would no longer need her.

Yet the desolation in her heart was real enough at the prospect ahead. Impossible to believe that she had known the governor for so short a time.

Suddenly a clearing opened before her, filled not with squalid huts but with dead flowers. They were several feet high, with bulbous, seed-pod heads. A man worked among them, extracting a sort of juice from the swollen heads, and in the center of the plot was an open shelter in which sat a couple of other laborers.

She stared, then suddenly realized what they were. She had seen dried flower heads like these before, on sale in Chiengmai by street vendors. They were empty opium poppy seed heads, milked of their contents. Poor laborers bought them to extract the last dregs of the narcotic from them.

Inadvertently she had stumbled on one of the illicit fields, hidden away in the hills.

The three men stared for a moment at this unexpected appearance, then one of them hurried away.

Suddenly she felt uneasy. These men could have no notion of who she was. The village where Father John had set up his clinic was much lower down, near the river. She was up here on her own, and could not speak a word of their strange tongue to explain her presence and her innocence.

Flight was the best course. She had wandered too far away from the village for safety, and now wanted only to get back to it.

Turning, she began to pick her way down the faint track, taking great care because a false step could bring disaster on the loose stones in the same way as Father John. If that happened, there was no one to help her here.

She had not gone many yards when there came the sound of a hurried descent behind her. A loose stone hurtled past her, and then a hand grasped her shoulder, forcibly detaining her. She glanced around in alarm to find herself face to face with Samrit Udom.

"Not so fast, my pretty nurse," he said smoothly. "Now that you have come so far and found a friend here in the shape of myself, you must come a little farther and see our tiny village. We have few visitors in so isolated a place, so you will be a novelty."

"You are no friend, and I've no wish to go any farther," she said with a conviction she did not feel. "I have a sick child in the lower village who needs my attention."

"So. Then why did you leave him and take this difficult climb? Was it to spy upon us?"

"Don't be absurd. I had no idea what was up here. I simply needed to get some fresh air after being forced to insert a tube into the child's throat to save him from choking. I've never done it on my own before, without proper facilities or any help. So it took it out of me, naturally."

"Then you're entirely alone at the village? I thought it strange, you being allowed to wander up here on your own. I had heard of the temporary clinic in the lower village but never dreamed we should see any of you this far up. We are well hidden."

He still grasped her shoulder. "I must go," she said again. "The child's mother will be expecting me."

"But she does not know which way you went," he said shrewdly, "and even if she did, could do nothing. They know better than to meddle with my affairs."

"Why didn't you come down and help us to stem the malaria outbreak? We could have used your skills," she said.

His laugh was scornful. "I'm finished with clinics, all of them. I only joined Father Joseph to learn all I could about pharmacy and drug processing. Now it is useful in the opium trade, and more remunerative than a dispenser's pay."

"Each to his own taste. Now let go my shoulder, please. The light is fading and I need to see on this atrocious track."

"You are coming with me. Accident or not, you have stumbled on our poppy field just at the crucial time when we are extracting the juice. Another few days and it will be all finished and the withered plants burned off, then it does not matter who sees. The evidence is gone."

Appalled, she gasped. "But you can't keep me against my will for several days."

Again he laughed. "You never did know me very well. Now come."

It was impossible to break away. His hand gripped her arm like a vise as he propelled her back up the slope. Anger and fear warred within her, but neither were of any help.

They reached the poppy field, crossed it, and came upon a few huts of the usual ramshackle appearance. One was bigger than the rest. To this he forced her.

"It will only be for a brief time, then you will be free to go," he said. "I shall be gone, far off, to turn my crop into many bahts. And don't think you can run away. Chaweewan is devoted to me and will do anything I say." He glanced at the girl, who now showed up in the dim light, and said a few words to her in that unknown hill tongue.

Chaweewan bundled her into one of the cupboardlike sleeping apartments.

"You may have it all to yourself," Udom called jeeringly. "I have a more appreciative girl now, so don't need to beg favors from you. And don't try anything so foolish as creeping off. My dog would be glad of the excuse to sink his teeth into you!"

The cur was eyeing her now, mangy and repulsive as they came. No, there was no escaping.

Left alone, she sank down on the straw bundle, her legs suddenly weak and useless. All of them would await her return in vain. The sick child and his mother, Father John with his sprained ankle, and in Chiengmai, Father Joseph, so busy and in need of her help.

CHAPTER ELEVEN

Father John was worried. Veena had been absent overnight and had not yet returned, even though the afternoon was far advanced. Still handicapped by his sprained ankle, which was both swollen and painful, he could do little himself, but had sent Chesda around to every hut in the village to see if anyone knew the woman who had called for help.

No one did. Communications between the small hill settlements were not good. Some of the people remained only for a short time, then moved on to build their flimsy homes on new ground, especially if they were involved in illicit opium growing.

These settlements had already been visited earlier when the medical team were trying to quell the malaria outbreak. On the second day of Veena's absence, Father John sent Chesda around them again to see if anything had been seen or heard of her.

Chesda returned in the late afternoon looking concerned and carrying Veena's canvas medical bag. He had found it in the home of the sick child to which she had been called. Being able to speak a few words of the language, he had discovered that Veena had performed a necessary operation on the child, then gone out for some fresh air. She had not returned as expected.

Father John looked grave. "I must get up there myself tomorrow, however painful. Apart from Veena's disappearance, the sick child may need further treatment," he said.

To his intense relief, a few minutes later David Lancaster turned up, accompanied by a trio of half-naked urchins directing him to the house of the white witch doctor.

"I've called as I promised, while I was at the lumber camp," he said. "How goes it? If your mission is finished, you may as well return with me. I'm off back to Chiengmai in the morning."

When Father John broke the news of Veena's disappearance, David let out an uncharacteristic oath, adding, "I never really approved of her coming in the first place. These hill tribes are not to be trusted. They've never really integrated with the Siamese, and defy the laws on opium growing. What are your own views, Father John? Do you think she wandered off and lost her way in the scrub, or what?"

"Possibly. The alternative is that she's being forcibly detained. I've seen many of these villagers smoking opium these past weeks, so its more than likely the poppies are being grown locally. If so, that sly dog Samrit Udom will have connections, since he's now left the clinic and is running an illegal racket with his father. He bears a grudge against Veena since she spurned his advances, so he'd be only too glad of an excuse to humiliate her, I feel sure."

"If not worse!" David growled. "My God, what will the governor say if she doesn't return! He believes she's simply working at the clinic, doesn't he?"

"That's right. He'll be out for blood. Stop his financial aid to the clinic maybe, and that would be disastrous. I'm going up to that village myself in the morning to see what I can find out. I can manage to communicate to a certain extent, thank God."

"I, too," David said. "I'll go with you. Two guns might be better than one, in the circumstances."

Accompanied by Chesda, they set out at daybreak the following morning, and soon reached the hut where he had found Veena's medical bag. While Father John attended to the child, David questioned the mother and several other villagers who had drifted up out of curiosity.

"One of them says he saw the white woman walking up the hillside," David reported when Father John had finished his ministrations. "He says there's a small community up there who have only been there for a few moons. They are an unfriendly bunch who don't encourage outsiders as they're growing opium poppies. At this time of year they'll no doubt be harvesting the juice, and then they'll probably move on to form a new encampment to avoid detection."

Father John nodded. "I deduced as much. We'll get up there immediately. I'm now convinced that Samrit Udom is involved in Veena's disappearance."

Although his ankle was not really fit for it, Father John in his anxiety made light of it and climbed doggedly up the rough slope. As expected, they presently came upon a patch of ground that had been cleared of undergrowth and planted with the forbidden crop. The harvesting was evidently just completed, for a couple of rough-looking laborers were setting fire to the dried-up remains of the poppies, and a pall of smoke hung over the ground.

Both David and Father John questioned the men, to no purpose. They merely shook their heads and declared they had seen no white woman.

"We'll search the huts before they move on," David said.

Their guns stifled any opposition. The sullen-looking occupants watched with expressionless faces as they glanced into each cramped sleeping apartment and open verandah, where tousle-headed offspring crawled around among dirty piglets and skinny hens.

When they reached the largest hut, they found it empty. No sign of food, cooking pots or the homespun blankets and clothes they used. Yet when David bent and touched the ashes of the fire on its stone bed, he found them still warm.

"Who lived in here?" he asked.

No one answered.

"I have means of making you talk."

When the gun was raised threateningly, one of the men volunteered. "Samrit Udom, but now he is gone with the harvest. We do not know where."

"He's probably right," Father John declared. "Udom is far too wily to leave easy trails to follow. And within a day or so this lot will vanish too with their livestock and chattels. They've planted no cotton or other crops, which means they only came to grow the poppies."

"How many women were with him?" David demanded. "You'd better tell the truth or you'll never leave here alive."

With a gesture of resignation, the man admitted that there were two.

"One tribal woman and one white stranger?"

"Yes."

"Such an arrangement could not continue for long," David said. "There'd be too much friction. Besides, Udom could never keep an easily identifiable girl like Veena for long against her will. Even in these wilds it would be difficult. My guess is that he'll let her go when he's gotten far enough away, and make for the labyrinths of Bangkok. Cash in on his illicit crop and enjoy the proceeds in his own murky way."

Father John looked slightly less despondent. "I hope to heaven you are right, but we can't bank on it. One thing seems clear, with the crop in his possession he would want quick transport, which among these hills means only the river."

"Did Samrit Udom make for the river?" he demanded of the man.

An unwilling nod confirmed their suspicions.

"Then he'll almost certainly have gone downstream toward Chiengmai, and from there hire faster transport to Bangkok. We'll follow first thing tomorrow, and hopefully find her back at the clinic," David deduced. "He's too shrewd to use violence against her and make himself a hunted man since the governor took her into his service."

Feeling rather more hopeful, they picked their way back to their camp and waited impatiently for the first gray light of dawn, when they hurried down to their boat and pushed off downriver.

Cool mist still lay over the water, but this soon dispersed as the sun rose higher, revealing the lush banks and the palms reaching out over the quiet waters.

"There's not much river traffic out here before the logging camp," David said. "We'll call in there and see if they noticed anything unusual in the way of passing boats yesterday."

Presently they reached the camp. A few boys were working among the mass of floating logs, lashing them together for when the rains came to swell the water into brisk spate and so facilitate their passage for Bangkok.

Chesda steered the boat toward the bank.

"Miss Basche, our nurse, has been abducted," he called. "Have you noticed any suspicious craft passing?"

Then, to the intense relief of David and Father John, there came an answering shout and Veena herself ran into view from the forest camp.

"I heard your voice," she called. "As welcome as an angel's. Bless you for coming to rescue me."

The three men landed, anxious to hear all about her ordeal over a brew of tea and a belated breakfast. They had been too concerned to eat before setting off, but now time was not so pressing.

"Are you all right and unharmed?" David asked, grasping both her hands and viewing her critically.

"Tolerable, if slightly itchy after that bug-ridden hut," she said. "Udom's woman kept at bay any designs he might have had on me, and a good bath in the river has cleared any lurking insects."

"How long have you been here?" Father John asked. "We searched the poppy field encampment yesterday but found you gone. We've been terribly worried about you."

"Udom guessed there'd be a search for me, so he left at dawn yesterday, taking only essentials. He went into hiding in the bush until he felt sure you'd have called off the search, then made his way down to the river at sundown, steering clear of the village where you had your clinic. He took one of the boats and with his two porters to navigate set off downriver. He dumped me overboard when we reached this camp and I had to wade ashore, while they carried on. There's no doubt he'll change to a more powerful boat at Chiengmai and be well on his way to Bangkok with his loot before we reach home. Once there, he can easily evade capture."

"So it seems that only your ill-fated climb up the hillside after attending to the child caused your unpleasant ordeal," David said. "It was not planned?"

"That's right. Until Udom had finished harvesting the poppies, he wasn't going to risk me fetching an armed gang of us up there, so he just hung on to me, hoping he'd be away with his spoils before a search party located the spot, and that's exactly what happened."

"Well, thank the blessed Virgin Mary you suffered nothing worse than discomfort," Father John declared. "The episode will mean we're back a little later than we had expected, and Father Joseph will be rushed off his feet."

And what of Taksin Chulasong, Veena thought with a pang. Almost certainly he would have returned to his palace before now. Was Sawitri also home from her visit and missing her? If so, there would be some awkward explaining to be done.

She was suddenly filled with anxiety and longing to be back. Only when they had returned to the boat and were speeding down to Chiengmai could she relax a little.

They reached the city in the heat of the afternoon and took samlors to the clinic. Here Father Joseph greeted them with obvious relief.

"I was beginning to feel worried," he said, "especially as there have been rumors that the Shans have been making raids over the borders into the hill country."

The Shans were from Burma, and as their own area of land had few natural resources, it was perhaps understandable that they should cast covetous eyes on the northern part of Siam, with its profitable ruby and silver mines and great teak forests. As the hill tribes already settled in the Siamese hills were of Burmese and Chinese extract, they had a bond of sympathy with the raiders and could not be relied on to take any action against them.

"We've had no trouble from that quarter," Father John said. "In fact, everything went very well until the last few days, when Veena found trouble which delayed us. And who do you think was responsible? None other than Samrit Udom."

The whole episode had to be related then. At the end of it, Father Joseph said, "The governor will no doubt be more angry than ever when he hears of it. He's hopping mad with me as it is, for letting you go off into the wilds, Veena."

She paled. "He's back from Bangkok then?"

"Oh yes. Several days ago. He called here, expecting you to be on the spot and available. As I said before, he was quite withering when he heard you'd gone on a mission. The repercussion might be a slashing of his patronage. Then we'll really be in trouble."

"I'd better go at once. I suppose it was wrong of me to let him believe I should be here helping out, but I knew if I told the full facts he would forbid it. I fully expected to be back before he was."

"Well, it cannot be helped. Don't upset yourself, my child. If he sends you packing in a rage, you will of course return here. As for any funds he might cut off, we'll have to cross that bridge when we reach it."

Outside the clinic she hailed a samlor and sat on tenterhooks as the cyclist peddled her toward the palace. How Samrit Udom would be laughing if he knew that his actions were causing this further trouble for her. May the Lord Buddha protect her from ever seeing his sly face again.

At the palace gate she paid off the samlor and hurried inside. How beautiful and how like coming home the gardens were after her absence. Leaving here finally would not be easy, but with the governor's marriage imminent, it seemed inevitable.

She followed the path around to the rear quarters and called Sawitri's name. The child was in the courtyard chasing a big bright butterfly, while Nada sat looking on.

Sawitri ran up and kissed her.

"Where have you been?" the child asked. "Nada had to look after me and she said she hoped you never would come back."

"She would. Well, now that I am back she can go in. I know she doesn't care much for being out of doors."

The woman strolled over, her expression belligerent.

"Oh no, Miss Basche. I am in charge at the moment. You are wanted by the governor. He commanded me to send you to him if I saw you."

It was useless to bandy words. Veena turned away, summoning up what courage she could. Had he been any ordinary employer, she would not have felt such apprehension. Dismissal would not have mattered greatly, since her former post was open and waiting for her. It was the personal involvement that caused her pulse to beat faster and her steps to falter. She felt too deeply about him to be able to take censure from him, yet face him she must.

He was in his study. A room that was exotic with oriental splendor yet Westernized to some degree with touches he had added, like his desk and capacious armchair. He sat in it now, looking every inch the distant scion of a royal house that he was in his midnight blue tunic embroidered with gold braid.

He did not rise to greet her in the courteous manner he usually showed toward her, but was very much the governor, to whom all kowtowed, as he sat regarding her with brooding anger.

She would not bow her head or make any other sign of submission. Darn him, she thought furiously. He could not treat her like an equal one day, uttering words that thrilled her to the core, and like a slave now, because she had not responded the moment he called. The little doll of a princess who would soon be his wife might glory in such doelike submission. She herself was made of sterner stuff.

"So you saw fit to put the work of the clinic before your position here," he said at last. "Worse still, you did not tell me the truth. You knew quite well about that mission into the hills, and equally well that I would have forbidden it. Do you call that loyalty?"

"Yes," she said bravely, "to my original calling. Malaria was scourging the hill people. They needed skilled help urgently, so I responded to the call. Had it not been for an unforeseen complication, I should have been back in Chiengmai before you."

"What complication?"

She told him then of what had occurred. At the mention of Samrit Udom he sprang from his chair and strode over to her, grasping her arms in a grip that hurt.

"Little fool, to put yourself at such risk for the sake of half-wild nomads. And it could have been much worse. The Shans have been raiding over the border, looting and killing any who opposed them. You could so easily have been killed, raped or carried off into slavery."

Her blue eyes opened wider, daunted by the fate she had narrowly missed.

"Yes!" he raged, actually shaking her in his anger. "I went through agonies when Father Joseph said you had gone to the hill country and were overdue back. I could have killed him for allowing you to do it. Now you'll make amends."

His arms slid around her and he was kissing her, not tenderly, with love, but with a wild passion that bruised her soft lips and seared her to the soul, making her a slave to his will. At first she tried to break away, conscious of the yawning gulf between them and the arrangements he had just completed to tie himself to another. But it was of no avail. His hold had the ruthlessness of an unleashed dam, and at last she gave up the struggle, hanging unresisting in his arms, until her own emotions caught fire, and answered his passion with equal ardor.

The tidal wave passed, leaving her spent and scarcely able to stand. He thrust her into his armchair and slumped on to the footstool beside it, head in hands.

"What are we to do?" he ground out as the silence lengthened.

"I must go back to the clinic. It is better so."

"No!" His voice was like an explosion. "How could I live without sight or sound of you, now that I have found the only woman who begins to compare with my dear lost one."

"But the situation would be impossible after you are married," she murmured. "It would not be fair to her, and unendurable to me."

"I know." His expression was deeply somber. "You can't know how it has haunted me these last weeks. I've thought and thought of a way out. On the journey to Bangkok I almost turned back, resolved to cancel any understanding with the princess's father, and beg you to marry me instead. That is what my heart clamors for."

"But your head says different, my lord. Neither your people nor the King would accept a commoner to bear a future ruler for them."

"That is true. It would mean renouncing my position and leaving the country to live in exile. A daunting thought, but one I would face, for you."

"But not I for you, lord. Nor for Sawitri. One day, when she

realized what she had lost, she would turn against me, and so
might you. How could I bear that?"

"Then we are in a cleft stick. There seems no way out, for I can
never let you go entirely."

"When is the marriage to be?" The words stuck in her throat.

"In one month's time, if I can bear to go through with it."

"Much can happen in a month." She hardly knew why she said
it. Wishful thinking perhaps.

"I can only pray that Lord Buddha in his wisdom will show me
the way."

"I too, my lord."

He rose, drawing her to her feet. "Now go to Sawitri. She will
be glad to have you back."

"I am pardoned, then?"

"Of course, but never deceive me again. Had it been anyone
else, I should have shown scant mercy."

For a moment she saw the conflict in his expression, the passion
that threatened to erupt again. Before he could give rein to it, she
broke away, with a hurried "I must go. Nada will be curious as to
why I linger so long. She considers me a usurper and would make
trouble if she could."

He snapped his fingers contemptuously. "She had better not
insult you or provoke me or she will be sent packing."

The baser side of her exulted in such sentiments, but common
sense urged caution. Malicious tongues spreading gossip could
harm those in high places, and she was determined that harm
should never befall this man or his child through her.

CHAPTER TWELVE

For once Veena tried to shut her ears to the temple bells making music, as the warm breeze shivered over the graceful towers of the wats. They seemed to herald the marriage of Taksin Chulasong, now looming near.

There was no escaping it in the crowded streets and parks of the old city. Workmen were busy everywhere, erecting poles to hold bunting and barriers to keep back the crowds who in ten days' time would gather to see the wedding procession. Already an air of festivity lay over the place. The common people welcomed spectacle of any kind and invariably made the most of it, having few other highlights in their drab lives.

"Don't dawdle, Sawitri. It's almost your bedtime," she said with more asperity than she usually showed toward the child. A battle raged continuously within her these days. Taksin still decreed that she must remain to care for Sawitri after his marriage, while she knew the impossibility of such a ménage.

Sawitri, her hot, sticky hand grasping the poke of honey candy Veena had bought for her, closed the gap between them. She was supremely happy, for they had just collected the pretty rose-pink satin gown she would wear at her father's wedding, and in it look as attractive as the bride herself.

They reached the palace gates and entered the grounds. The peace and calm was balm to Veena's soul. She glanced toward the lake in passing and there, gazing at the poignant statue, was Taksin Chulasong.

He must have heard his daughter's piping voice, for he strode across and joined them as they walked around to the back regions. Veena had the impression that he had been waiting for her return.

"How would you like to accompany me on a day-long trip to Si Satchanalai tomorrow?" he asked, including them both in his sweeping glance. "The ruins have so recently been discovered that some of them have not yet been excavated."

Sawitri clapped her hands, clamoring to go, but Veena said nothing. Her heart was beating too thickly.

Taksin added, for her benefit only, "I have decided to embark on a short history of Siam, something I have long considered writing. It will be a welcome intellectual escape later on, to speak plainly. As you probably know, Sukhothai was the first capital of Siam, from the thirteenth century to the fourteenth, when the honor passed to Ayutthaya. It was an extensive and magnificent city, and so was Si Satchanalai, where the Crown Prince had his residence and governed. I need to see it first-hand, and now is a good time before coming events enmesh me too deeply. I think it might be interesting for Sawitri to see the ruins, and you too, Miss Basche."

He still used the formal address, even after that one wild surge of passion. All too conscious, perhaps, of ears ever open for scandal in his vulnerable position.

"It sounds a most worthwhile project, my lord," she said at last, "and as the prospect of a day out pleases Sawitri, I am ready to accompany her."

"You might sound a little more enthusiastic," he said as they reached the private courtyard by the schoolroom suite. "The river trip alone, to and from the site, should be a pleasure in this sultry weather."

"Of course. It is good of you to include us." For the life of her, she could not help the stiffness, fearful lest the clamoring excitement within her should bubble to the surface and show too clearly. A whole day with him away from the palace sounded like heaven, but surely they would be treading a razor's edge.

"Then please retire early. We must be up at dawn. My boat will be ready and waiting for us with lunch aboard," he said.

Rising early was not difficult, as in her anticipation Veena had scarcely slept. Sawitri, too, was awake very early and almost too excited to eat breakfast. They found two rickshaws waiting outside.

The governor seated himself in the first and was borne off toward the river, while Veena and the child followed.

Orange-robed monks were much in evidence at this early hour, walking in file with their begging bowls. Their lives were austere and restrictive, but as they were not required to stay longer than three months in the monasteries if they did not wish to, this period was not too demanding. Even princes and governors accepted it in their youth as a necessary part of life, to learn discipline and humility and please Lord Buddha, so gaining merit.

They reached the Ping River and there embarked. The boat had been specially constructed for the governor's use, to facilitate any travels, and was a modified small yacht, steam-engine fitted. A canopy covered the deck in the stern, beneath which were seats and cushions to form a comfortable observation lounge. Here Taksin Chulasong, Veena and Sawitri settled themselves, while the two crew members busied themselves at the engine in the bow.

Soon they were off, speeding their way south, passing lumbering rice barges, longboats and small boats piled with produce. This was the most enjoyable time of day, before the sun climbed high, bringing shimmering heat with perspiration and lassitude in its wake.

"Does the river take us all the way?" Veena asked.

"Yes. We leave the Ping presently and take a connecting klong that links with the Yom River. This flows directly past ruined Si Satchanalai."

It was a delightful journey. Sawitri trailed her fishing line in the water and actually caught a fish. Veena was content to lean back, simply absorbing the rural tranquillity and storing up these golden moments for later days when such idylls would be impossible. Taksin Chulasong, conscious no doubt of his crew, spoke only desultorily and inconsequentially, but frequently. Although not looking directly at him, Veena felt his dark eyes turned intently toward her face, and knew that he, too, was storing up memories for the future.

When Sawitri plaintively declared that she was hungry, Veena spread out the contents of their picnic basket on a white cloth and they feasted on cold chicken, rice, fruit and little cakes, washed down by fruit drinks and tea. Then, as the remains were packed away, Taksin glanced ahead and declared that they had reached their goal in its quiet backwater.

They drew into the bank. "I shall not require your assistance," Taksin told the two crew members. "Stay and keep an eye on the boat. We shall be gone for several hours."

They stepped ashore, and almost instantly the trees and bushes that had sprung up unchecked over the years enveloped them. They were in an enchanted world of their own, away from prying eyes and listening ears.

A brief walk brought them to the ruined site, a wide expanse of baked sandy soil from which rose the remains of a once flourishing city. Graceful spires of chedis soared into the sky, defying time and the ravages of nature. Crumbling walls and fallen masonry of great wats hedged them in. Broken Buddhas sat serenely in the lotus pose, contemplating man and his futility as they had done for centuries.

Some of these structures were half-obliterated by time and the creeping jungle, their outlines blurred with festooning vines and withered grass. Bushes sprang from some of them, and encroaching trees softened the harsh stones left standing, gauntly defiant.

Taksin Chulasong drew in his breath. "Imagine it as it once was," he said, "when a prince ruled here over monks and all his subjects. See those amazing broken elephants over there! That was the Wat Chang Lom. I'm hoping to restore them to their original perfection if I can stir the authorities into action, and excavate the whole site. It will take time and money, but one day it will be finished, if I have my way."

"I want to see the elephants!" Sawitri raced over the uneven ground to the enormous creatures.

"Take care of the fallen stones," called her father.

He whipped out his notebook and began to write furiously, while Veena followed the child.

The elephant remains were enormous. Built of rough bricks,

they still stood squarely, defying time. Minus trunks, ears and their outer casing of smooth plaster, they were still easily identifiable as the lovable lords of the jungle, friends and helpers of man.

"They'll look marvelous if they can be restored," Veena said as Taksin joined them.

He nodded. "The whole site is well worth saving, before the jungle takes over entirely and it is lost forever. It will be almost as impressive as the Ayutthaya ruins when carefully excavated and a little restoration done."

Ayutthaya. The ancient capital whose ruins had ages ago been the setting for Chantra's brief hour of fulfillment. Veena tried to visualize the poignant young ancestor of so long ago, whose only link was a yellowing faded notebook of neat script.

"This is even older, of course," he went on. "Apart from being the residence of the Crown Prince, it had another claim to fame. Very fine pottery was made here in kilns to the north of the city. It was sent all over Siam and much prized. We have some of the *sawankhalok* ware at my palace to this day."

"I wonder why the city eventually declined," Veena mused.

"The same reason as Ayutthaya. The incessant wars with the people of the north, chiefly the Burmese. They brought death and destruction to much of Siam, and now, unfortunately, the Shans are threatening us again, at least in the north."

Veena sighed.

"Enough of introspection!" he said, putting away his notebook. "We are here to enjoy ourselves. Let us simply wander over the site and try to imagine it as it once was."

That was pleasant enough on this warm afternoon, in the silence and solitude. Ancient frangipani trees grew here and there among the broken columns, scenting the air as they had long ago scented the temples. Lizards basked on the fallen stones, and unseen birds called from the soaring spires in place of the wind bells of old.

Inevitably Sawitri, unused to such liberty, wore herself out, and complained that she was tired and thirsty.

Her father smiled indulgently on her. "You've done very well.

We'll find a suitable place and rest for a while. I have a few mandarin oranges in my pocket from the picnic basket."

"Oh goody!" Sawitri found a grassy bank hemmed in by broken walls, sunny and secluded. "A nice little house," she said.

They threw themselves down. The oranges were peeled and eaten, after which the child curled up like a kitten, face shaded by her sun hat, and drifted off to sleep.

Veena felt a great desire to follow suit, but for the constraint that now filled her. Not since that brief interlude in his study, when he had held and kissed her with such passion, had they been virtually alone.

"This day is ours," he said at last. "One to remember when irksome ties bind me to another. Buddha in his infinite compassion has taken pity on us and cast his blessing upon us. For this brief moment we can forget everything that stands between us and savor it to the full."

He took her perfect face between his hands and turned it toward him.

"You are like the frangipani blossoms, fragile yet enduring, simple yet infinitely beautiful. Are you afraid, my perfect one, or have you the courage to grasp what is offered? Together we could soar to a paradise such as you have never yet known, and I have almost forgotten. Are you afraid?"

"No," she murmured. "How could I fear anything with you?"

His lips met hers, as gently as a falling petal. He drew her down beside him and they lay in the drowsy silence, savoring the delight of such nearness to the full. Kissing, caressing, murmuring words of endearment and sighs of pure bliss.

His hands on her body set her shuddering with desire. Deep waves of passion seared through her, urgent and insatiable as a forest fire. Now there was no turning back. Gasps of pure delight escaped her lips and she almost wept with her frantic need of him. The need to be wholly and completely one with him, there under the torrid sun.

His teasing ceased, his desire as great as hers. She felt the warm weight of him above her, rock hard yet sustaining. His hot breath mingling with hers, his face rough against her own.

Pain and ecstasy intermingled in this strange new paradise. She left mortals behind and reached Nirvana, the ultimate experience. For the first time, she soared with him to a height she had never dreamed existed.

Afterward she still clung to him. How could she ever let him go after this, and see him married to another?

As though he divined her thoughts, he said, "Even now it is not too late. I could renounce everything, for you."

"And be an outcast forever. An exile from your country. Oh no, I could never live with that. It would destroy all chance of happiness for us and rob Sawitri of her birthright."

He sighed deeply. Already the outer world was encroaching with its duties and responsibilities. Truly man was born to unhappiness for the good of his soul, as the priests in the temples taught. Joy could not last for more than a brief moment in an ocean of time.

The sun was now in a descending arch, the hush of late afternoon lay over the forgotten city. They had already lingered longer than prudence decreed.

"We must go," he said with reluctance, "but our hearts will forever remain here in this enchanted world."

Sawitri stirred, yawned and sat up. They, too, rose and tidied themselves and almost in silence they walked back to where the boat was waiting.

Darkness overtook them halfway back. The river gleamed blackly about them and fireflies flashed in bright streaks above it. From the jungle came strange harsh calls of night birds and an occasional chilling roar of a four-footed hunter, as they reached their boat and embarked.

It was late when at last they drew in to a landing stage at Chiengmai. Long past Sawitri's bedtime. Yet even at this hour they had no difficulty in finding a couple of samlors, their owners glad to earn a few bahts.

With the streets now free of oxcarts and such unwieldy traffic, they were pedaled swiftly on their way to the palace. The coolies were paid off, and it was time to part. Taksin Chulasong naturally turned to the front door, but touched Veena's hand in passing, with a murmured "I would give much if you could take dinner with me. As that is impossible, good night, my dear one, and roam with me in dreams through the lost cities of the past."

Her heart full of conflicting emotions, Veena took the child's hand and walked quickly to their rear suite.

Nada was sitting there waiting for them. In the way of Eastern servants, she knew all about the long day's trip—just the governor, his daughter and Veena together—and no doubt was full of suspicious, jealous disapproval.

"It grows late," she said sourly. "Too long a day for the small one. She will be overtired. Come, my blossom, Nada will undress you and put you to bed!"

"I'm not tired at all," Sawitri piped. "We found a lovely ruined city where there was no one but us. I fell asleep and slept for ages."

The woman stared from her to Veena with her sharp black eyes. Veena could sense the suspicions racing through her narrow mind. Imagine the scurrilous whispers she would set going in the palace, if it suited her, unless she valued the governor's good name, and hated only her rival for the child's affections.

"I'll put Sawitri to bed myself," she said. "You may bring a tray of light refreshments for us both."

Nada seemed about to argue, then turned on her heels and went.

It took only a few minutes before the little girl was sitting up in her small bed, mosquito net neatly folded on the frame above ready to be let down. By this time Nada was back with a loaded tray.

She set a glass of some light fruit drink and a plate of little rice cakes on the bamboo table by the bed, then held out the rest to Veena.

There was cold fish, rice, fruit and a pot of coffee.

"I made the coffee specially for you myself, since the kitchen staff are busy with the governor's dinner," she said with unwonted generosity. "I thought you might prefer it to a cold drink."

Veena summoned a smile. "That was kind of you. No, I'll not keep you up any longer. Good night, and thanks."

While Sawitri satisfied her hunger, Veena merely picked at her own food, too strung up by the shattering events of the day to feel hungry. Thirst was another matter. She could have downed the contents of the coffee pot with alacrity, yet some vague unease deterred her. Why had Nada, usually so truculently obstructive toward her, troubled to make coffee for her instead of doling out a fruit drink as for the child? It made no sense.

With the mosquito net securely tucked in around the small bed, Veena carried the tray to her own room. She poured out a little of the coffee and sniffed at it.

Was there a strange odor about it, or was it merely her over-wrought imagination? Better to leave it than risk an upset diges-tion. Deliberately she poured all of it down the soak-away in the primitive Eastern bathroom and drank instead the boiled water from the carafe kept for teeth-cleansing purposes.

The following morning, in a half-conscious state between sleep-ing and waking, she sensed that someone had entered the room. Opening her eyes, she saw Nada standing by the bamboo table on which the tray stood, peering into the coffee pot. The discovery that it was empty seemed to please her, for she smiled as she returned the lid.

But on approaching the bed and seeing Veena staring at her, the woman's expression changed to surprised vexation.

"Are you feeling all right?" she asked.

"Of course. Why not?"

"Did the coffee please you? You drank it all?"

Veena decided to test her out. "No. I fancied it had a strange odor."

"What did you do with it?" Surely there was a note of appre-hension in the voice.

"I poured it away so that it could do no harm to anyone."

"Why should coffee harm anyone? Are you accusing me of trying to poison you?"

"No, just strongly suspecting it. Your odd behavior this morn-ing adds weight to my theory. You don't usually come in so early, and as you've brought no tea, just why did you come, if not to see if I had conveniently expired?"

Nada's face contorted with rage and fear. "Would that you had!" she spat out. "You are an evil influence here, on the child and on her father."

"Get out," Veena ordered. "I shall ask for someone else to serve the nursery suite in future, since I can no longer trust you."

After she had gone Veena rose, debating her next move. She decided that it would be wise to put the matter in Taksin's hands and let him decide the issue.

The question was, how could she catch him alone? After his day off yesterday, he would be extremely busy on administrative duties and preparations for the wedding. She doubted if he would find time to call in at the schoolroom as he formerly did. Then she recalled his passion for fitness. Ever since his youth, following the Western fashion, he had kept up as far as possible a routine of exercise, and this no doubt had maintained his superb physique.

A rear, secluded part of the palace grounds, adjoining the schoolroom courtyard, was reserved by him for his own use. Here in the early morning he practiced physical culture whenever he could. There happened to be a door that opened between them. It was usually kept locked and she had never ventured to turn the key herself.

Now she did just that, and was relieved to find him in nothing more than a pair of shorts running steadily around the confined space.

He stopped in surprise when he saw her.

"*Saw-a-dee.* It is indeed a pleasure to see you, but is it wise, my lotus blossom? Who knows what prying eyes are upon us even now."

"I know, and only expediency prompts the indiscretion, my lord."

As briefly as possible, she related the events of the last few hours, adding, "Doubtless, Nada is fanatically loyal to you and Sawitri and bears you no ill will, but me she deeply resents as a usurper and a disruptive influence. I fear she would stop at nothing to be rid of me."

Taksin frowned. "She must go. I cannot allow you to remain

under threat a moment longer. Never fear. She will be sent packing this very morning."

To emphasize his point, he grasped her shoulder with a reassuring hand. It seemed to burn through her thin blouse, sending shock waves of fire darting through her. His naked, sunburned chest with its sun-bleached hair was so close that she was forced to clench her hands at her sides to prevent herself reaching out and touching him with caressing fingers.

And the ardent lips that had kissed her so passionately yesterday among the ruins were so dangerously near that she had to break away with a breathless: "I had better go back. Sawitri will be awake and looking for me."

He felt her conflict. It was in him, too. Yet in spite of the power of his exalted position, he could only stand and watch her go. For there could be no compromise. It was all or nothing. Either he renounced everything for himself and his child and snatched what happiness he could with his new love in exile or face up to what the King and the people of Chiengmai expected of him, which was self-effacing duty, a marriage of convenience and the production of a son to carry on tradition.

He sighed deeply. At that moment he would gladly have exchanged places with one of the rickshaw coolies if it meant that he could do exactly as he pleased, without betraying a bond of honor and branding himself a coward.

CHAPTER THIRTEEN

Veena's mind was not on the lesson she was giving to Sawitri. How could she focus her attention on the wildlife of Siam when it constantly wandered to matters nearer home. The marriage of Taksin, creeping ever nearer, the disturbing rumors of the Shans massing on the northern borders and the harassing of isolated outposts, the nonappearance of the Lancaster children this morning for their usual schoolroom session.

It had been several days since she had seen them. Possibly they were ill. It would set her mind at rest to go and see for herself.

So to Sawitri's delight, they put away their books and set off in a samlor for the riverside bungalow of the Lancasters. Veena found them in the garden, the children playing with their dolls, while Selina lounged in a shaded bamboo chair looking pale and anxious.

"I hope your migraine isn't bothering you, my dear," Veena said. "I called to inquire why the children didn't come as usual this morning."

"That's good of you, Veena. I'm not ill, though I soon shall be if this goes on much longer. I just could not bear to be left on my own, so kept the children with me."

"Why, what's happened?" Veena asked with concern. "Has David had an accident or something?"

"I don't know. That's the worry. He should have been back home the day before yesterday, but never turned up, and still there's no word. He's up-country somewhere, and one never knows exactly where, or if anything is amiss. It could merely be

that one of the elephants is sick and he's staying with it, but with
these rumors of trouble with the Shans, one never knows."

Veena frowned in concentration. "It might be wise to come
back to the palace with me and report the situation to the governor. He's very understanding, and I'm sure will help in any way
he can. These teak camps are under his protection, after all, and
having telegraph equipment in the palace, he might be able to find
out something."

"If you really think he won't mind being bothered at a time like
this with his marriage imminent, I'll be glad to come," Selina
agreed. "I'll go crazy if I stay worrying alone much longer."

So she and the children accompanied Veena back, and Taksin
Chulasong granted her an audience before lunch.

She looked slightly less worried when she rejoined Veena and
the children.

"The governor says we are to lunch with you and Sawitri while
his secretary telegraphs around to see what he can discover," she
said. "The courthouse of the teak company at Sankam is linked
up to Chiengmai and they may possibly know something. So is the
main camp, but that's the only one at present."

"Sankam's farther north, not all that far from the border,"
Veena said thinking uneasily of the Shans.

"That's right. Central for the teak and elephant camps. A great
deal of business is done there, and David does go there quite
frequently to draw wages for the elephant boys and logging men."

Which meant they would keep considerable sums of money on
the premises. A tempting prospect for an invading horde, if they
were desperate and bold enough.

Lunch was brought in to them soon after and they ate it with
faces as cheerful as they could manage, then soon after Taksin
Chulasong himself came in, looking disturbed.

"I'm afraid the news, what little we could find out, is not
good," he told Selina. "My secretary got through to the main
camp. They said Nai Lancaster had been, but had left the following day, believed to be bound for the teak courthouse in Sankam."

"And is he there?" Selina asked urgently.

Taksin shook his head. "At first my secretary could make no

contact with anyone at all at the courthouse. After repeated tries, a minor official got on the line. He said a large number of Shans had raided the place, some of them armed with stolen guns. They'd killed all five of the courthouse staff except he himself, who was wounded in the leg, and made off with all the cash they could lay hands on and anything else that took their fancy."

"And what of David?" Selina asked in agony.

"They apparently waylaid and captured him on his way to the courthouse. He was with them, his hands trussed behind his back. As they had not killed him like the Siamese officials, they may be holding him for possible ransom, he being English."

Selina released a long breath. "Well, that's something, I suppose, but bad enough. What can we do?"

"This is a serious matter," Taksin said grimly. "You must leave it to me. I feel responsible for the teak company, your husband and you and your children. You will remain in the palace with Miss Basche for the present. This is best for your safety. It's unlikely that marauders will dare to enter our city, but one can never be certain. I've just learned that a ruby mine in the foothills was attacked and all the uncut jewels stolen. That is not far away."

"I don't suppose these raiding gangs will encounter much opposition from the hill people," Veena said. "After all, they are of similar origin, and the hill people already hostile because of the government's opposition to their opium growing. Such men as Samrit Udom and his father will be all too ready to urge on the rebels, now that they're already wanted men."

Taksin nodded. "True enough. What they would like is an entirely separate state in the north, unanswerable to any laws made in Bangkok. If many more cross the border, things will look very serious indeed. We must try to stop them now if we can."

"You mean to send in troops?" Veena said.

"Indeed. This latest outrage of kidnaping Nai Lancaster enables me to act on my own initiative, although my forces are limited. Our small garrison comprises no more than seventy-five men, soldiers and gendarmes. I can send for help, of course, but it will be a long time in getting here from Bangkok."

Veena shook her head ruefully. "This trouble couldn't have

come at a worse time for you with the marriage imminent. You carry too many burdens, my lord."

He shrugged. "The marriage is of little importance compared with the pillaging of my domain. Perhaps they consider it an opportune moment to run riot while my attention is on other matters. They'll soon see we are not to be trifled with."

His orders went out. The troops began to prepare themselves with weapons, stores, mules and elephants to carry the loads. On the second day they were ready, and marched at dawn to wreak revenge for killings and lootings and to try to rescue David Lancaster, if they could find him.

"Who knows where he is now," Selina lamented. "No doubt they've hidden him somewhere. It will be like looking for a needle in a haystack in that wild hill country."

Privately Veena agreed, but she tried to rally her friend's spirits to the best of her ability. She was glad to have Selina and the children with her, as it kept her from brooding too much on the coming ceremony. She saw almost nothing of Taksin, who was too preoccupied with one thing and another. A number of minor royal connections had been invited, together with the few foreign diplomats in this northern province. He was conscious of the inadequacy of the handful of gendarmerie left in the city to guard these dignitaries while in procession. Although he did not anticipate any attack on a city as large as Chiengmai, he nevertheless borrowed what trained men he could to patrol the streets and keep watch, but they were far too few.

As day succeeded day, both Veena and Selina grew more and more desperate. Veena could not bear the thought of watching the ceremony that would cut off Taksin completely from any legitimate contact with her, while Selina began to fear she would never see David again. Reports of minor raids on various small towns and villages in the vicinity filtered through to add to their worries. Siamese men, women and children were being brutally killed by the invading Shans, their domestic animals stolen and homes looted.

The much-needed military help from the south did not materialize. Even a small army, with all its equipment needing to be transported by mules or elephants, would take weeks to arrive, Taksin told Veena on one of their rare, brief meetings. A detachment had been sent by river, but even that could not hope to reach Chiengmai before the wedding ceremony. As for the force sent out by Taksin to rout the invaders and discover news of David, nothing was heard of them for several days.

Then, just two days before the wedding ceremony, a mere trickle of them came limping back into the city, some wounded, and minus supplies, animals, ammunition and everything. In dismay, Taksin hurried out to the forecourt of the palace, where they had assembled to report their failure to the governor.

"What happened?" he demanded.

The officer being killed, one of the men stepped forward. His story went that after several days' fruitless searching, they heard that Nai Lancaster was being held in a village not far off. The way lay through a narrow ravine between two hills. They set off on the march, but when they were halfway through, a gong sounded somewhere on the heights, and from both in front and behind a yelling mob hurled themselves forward, brandishing every kind of weapon, including guns. Most of the governor's luckless force were killed or too badly wounded to make their escape. A few managed to conceal themselves in the undergrowth on the hillsides until all their attackers had gone, taking with them stores, ammunition and animals. These few then made their way back to Chiengmai as fast as they could, and here they were.

The governor looked grim. "There seems little else we can do until reinforcements arrive," he said to Selina, who with Veena had followed him to the forecourt to glean news. "We cannot even be sure that your husband is in fact being held in the village mentioned as rumored, or if it was merely a trick to lure my force into that vulnerable position in the ravine. I suspect that was the case, as the rebels were all set to pounce when the moment was ripe. Ambush is all too easy in hill country."

Selina nodded miserably, very near to tears. Veena comforted her to the best of her ability, while Taksin assured her that a fresh search party would be sent out immediately as soon as sufficient reinforcements arrived to make it worthwhile.

"If it is any comfort," he added, "I hardly think the invaders will harm such a valuable hostage. They would be much more likely to hold him for ransom."

So another day and night passed, the city outside assuming a more and more festive air, while inside the palace an uneasy expectation reigned. Veena longed to escape before she was forced to witness the actual ceremony that would tear Taksin from her, but felt powerless to defy him and desert Sawitri before then. Afterward, with the little doll princess to assume care of the child, she herself would beg him to let her go, before her heart broke with frustrated longing.

And now here was the very day before the wedding ceremony. The day when the bride, her father and retinue would arrive in Chiengmai in procession, to be there in good time for the rituals of the following day. A suite of rooms in the palace had been prepared for them, and the servants scurried around like busy ants, even though the guests were not expected until midafternoon.

Veena felt like a person under sentence of death. It was fortunate that Selina, who knew nothing of the situation between Veena and Taksin, was too preoccupied with her own fears for David to really notice her friend's withdrawn sadness. To have brought it out into the open would only have made Veena feel worse.

The morning dragged. Afternoon came, and with it excitement for Sawitri. She flatly refused to take a siesta in case she missed the arrival of the princess, and raced around, chattering and singing, until she almost drove Veena mad.

But when the sun sank low, and still there was no sign of the guests, even her expectation began to wane.

"I shall not go to bed until the princess is here," she declared. "Why doesn't she hurry?"

Her resolution was never tested, for, just as the short dusk was falling, and everyone else in the palace was beginning to wonder what had happened to the travelers, a most wonderful surprise burst on Selina.

There was a knock on the door that opened into the courtyard, and on opening it, Veena found herself confronting a man in tattered, dirty clothes, a week's growth of beard, unkempt hair and face caked with sweat and blood from jungle scratches.

She stared in disbelief for a moment until he said, "So I've found the right entrance. I wasn't sure. I called at the bungalow and was told Selina and the children were here."

With a wild cry of "David!", Selina flung herself across the room and into his arms, laughing and crying at the same time in a burst of hysteria. Vicky and Sally followed, clinging to his legs so that he could not move.

"This is wonderful," Veena said, "but let the poor man get inside. He looks badly in need of a bath, rest and food, and I'm sure he has a thrilling tale to tell us."

"Thrilling is hardly the word," he said grimly, as Selina drew him inside. "Horrific is more like it. I must see the governor at once."

"Wouldn't it be better to clean up a bit first?" she faltered. "He is waiting to receive important guests. The bridal party, in fact."

"I know. That's why I must speak to him immediately. Will you find out exactly where he is, Veena?"

He was in deadly earnest. Some new calamity was about to descend on them, she realized with sinking heart as she rang for a servant.

"Please tell the governor that Nai Lancaster is here and has something very urgent to tell him," she instructed the servant. "Ask if Nai Lancaster may come to his study."

The servant departed to return quite quickly with the governor himself in his wake.

"My dear fellow, I'm indeed glad to see you, even in such a sorry state," he said. "Tell me how you escaped and all you can about the invaders and then my man will look after you in the way of a bath and fresh clothes."

"The Shans have crossed the border in large numbers," David said, "and many of the hill people have joined them. A group of the latter led by Samrit Udom abducted me and kept me prisoner for the sole purpose, I surmise, of drawing a force of militia from Chiengmai to search for me, leaving the city without adequate cover for their attack."

"They mean to attack?"

"Without question, my lord. They consider that now, with the city in festive mood, is a perfect time. I heard some of them talking last night before I managed to get my hands free and escape. I tried desperately to reach the bridal procession in time, but having no transport and being obliged to keep under cover I was just too late."

"Too late for what?" Taksin's voice was grim.

"The procession was ambushed halfway here, my lord. Most of them were killed, including the bride and her father, and all their possessions, including transport, stolen. I witnessed most of it from concealment at the edge of the jungle. There was nothing at all I could do, except push on here and break the news, after they'd gone with their loot, also warn you of the attack on the city. It will almost certainly come tomorrow."

"Our city under attack, with only a handful of men to guard it." Taksin spoke like a man in the middle of a nightmare. "I must get through to Bangkok immediately and let them know the full extent of our danger. You, of course, will remain here with your family."

Not a word of his assassinated bride, Veena reflected. Was he too stunned to speak of it, or was there an element of relief that at this eleventh hour, fate had stepped in and freed him from a yoke he had neither sought nor wanted?

Yet it could make no real difference to the barrier that lay between herself and Taksin, she thought sadly. It would only mean a delay before someone else must be chosen. For the governor must produce an heir by a bride acceptable to the King and the people, and under no circumstances would she, a commoner, be considered acceptable.

Try as she might, she could not keep out a touch of envy as she glanced at David and Selina, absorbed in each other to the exclusion of everyone else.

CHAPTER FOURTEEN

Would the dawn never come?

Only the children in the entire palace had slept at all. The rest had been busy preparing for flight, since without adequate forces a city of this size could not be defended against an advancing horde.

The King himself had ordered it. Taksin had contacted him the previous evening with the news of the imminent invasion, the assassination of the bridal party, the outrages and looting of the teak courthouse, ruby mine and other centers, and the rampaging hordes of Shans pouring over the northern border. The King had replied that for the moment retreat was the only way to avoid further loss of life, until the advancing army he had sent could reach and liberate the city, and protect the teak companies' properties and mines.

"The royal barge is big enough to carry us all to Bangkok, including you," Taksin told David, "for, having just escaped from the enemy, they'll show no mercy to you and your family if they lay hands on you again. You must come with me."

Just before dawn he sent two servants loaded with provisions to alert the crew and tell them to be ready to sail at a moment's notice. A shock lay in store when the two returned with the news that a party of Shans had infiltrated downriver in the night, killed the crew and made off with the barge in the direction of the north from which they had come.

They were roused from their stunned shock by a palace servant who reported a great fire burning just outside the White Elephant Gate, the main outlet of the city northward. Rushing out into the grounds, they could see the lurid flames leaping up in a fearful display of power gone mad.

"No escape that way, but then we should never have gone north with more and more of them massing there," Taksin said. "There are three other gates."

The inner, or old, city was built roughly like a square surrounded by high walls. A gate at each point of the compass gave the only outlets. Now, with the enemy about to burst in upon them, the whole city seemed to be on the move, intent on escape.

From the palace gates the people could be seen swarming by. With bundles on backs, rickshaws and carts piled high with prized possessions, they passed, young men carrying aged parents, mothers with children strapped around them. Asses brayed, children screamed, men cursed those in front for moving too slowly. The whole scene was one of panic and despair.

"They're obviously making for the East Gate and the Ping River," David said. "It offers the best chance of escape, since the others lead only to poor roads passing through jungles. However, it's a safe bet to assume the Shans have placed a guard on it after capturing the royal barge. They'll be determined not to let you escape, my lord, carrying the cream of your jewels, no doubt, even if they let the common people through. Both you and I are too well-known to hope to get through, unless we can disguise ourselves."

Taksin nodded grimly. "Ragged servants' clothes, bare feet and rough bundles, that's the only way we can hope to elude capture. Your face is sunburned enough to pass if you wear a coolie hat and dark glasses, but your wife and children will have to be dyed brown and wear Siamese dress."

Veena immediately set to work with camouflage on Vicky, Sally and Selina. Old clothes were dug out for them all, and soon they presented a fair picture of two adult Siamese males with their wives and three children.

"All we can take with safety is bundles of food and some money hidden on our persons," Taksin said, glancing with resignation at the splendor around them.

"What of your gold and treasures, my lord?" Veena asked with a sigh.

"I think I've foiled them in that respect, to some extent. I spent two hours last night with my most trusted servant, gathering the best and transporting them where neither barbarians can steal or fire destroy them. Deep under the palace is a cellar where ice is kept through the hot weather to preserve food. They are securely locked in there. When this horror is over, something will be left to help rebuild the past, even if they burn down the palace, as they probably will."

If only she could be the one to help rebuild the past with him, Veena reflected with a sigh, but that was just a pipe dream. Perhaps none of them would survive even.

Urged on for their own safety by the governor, the palace staff now melted away before the advancing Shans, arrived to pillage and murder. Taksin and his party prepared to follow, the former with deep reluctance. Veena had the distinct impression that had there been no others save himself to consider, he would never have abandoned his imposing home, but like the captain of a sinking ship, would have remained with it to the bitter end, even at the cost of his own life.

Emerging onto the front courtyard, they came face-to-face with one of the palace gardeners arriving at his usual time for his morning's work. His normal smiling good humor was lacking. Now he looked scared out of his wits as he burst out, "May the Lord Buddha preserve us, my lord! The Shans have burned down the White Elephant Gate and are pouring into the city. An advance mob has stormed the jail and released the prisoners from their chains. They have joined the invaders to loot, burn and kill. We shall all perish."

"You will if you remain here," his master told him. "Go as the other servants have. There should be time yet for you to escape before they overrun the entire city and perhaps seal the gates. Hide in the jungle until the army from Bangkok arrives to drive out the invaders."

Wringing his hands, the gardener scurried off. David urged the party to follow, reflecting wryly that surely no Shan would con-

nect this ragged, barefoot little band with the illustrious governor
or the influential Englishman so well-known in the teak business.
Straw hats and sunglasses obscured their features, while Selina's
fair hair was covered with a scarf like the children's.

"It is galling having to leave horses and every other means of
transport and walk," Taksin said as they set off, "but the poorer
and meaner we look, the more chance we have of getting out of
the city without question or detention. If we can reach the river,
we'll hope to hire a boat, although they'll probably be at a premium now, with everyone who can afford it having the same
idea."

Just how great was the need for speed became apparent as soon
as they left the palace grounds. The road was still congested with
people, animals, carts and cycles, which had the advantage of
giving the palace party cover. In their squalor, they merged perfectly with the scurrying crowd. Only close scrutiny would reveal
their deception, and unless they were unlucky, they were scarcely
likely to be singled out.

With Sawitri clinging to Veena's hand and the two Lancaster
children clutching their mother's faded pasin, they pushed ahead
as fast as they could. While passing the various temples beside the
road, they could hear the chanting of prayers ascending to Buddha, beseeching him to save their wats, built in his name.

The east or Tape Gate came into view. It stood wide, with a
guard on either side. They had strongly Mongol features and were
clearly vanguards of the oncoming horde. Taksin halted his party,
in order to observe how freely they were allowing the crowds to
pass.

"They are making no arrests," he said presently, "so presum-
ably they have orders to let the people go, providing they make no
trouble. What they are after is anything of value left behind in the
city and wats. Any who have remained and try to oppose them
will be slaughtered without compunction."

David nodded, his glance on a man whose way was suddenly
barred by the sword of one of the guards. The man was better
dressed than most and leading a mule with side panniers piled

with bundles. Taller than most Siamese, he was in fact not much shorter than Taksin himself.

The second guard joined in the interrogation which followed. Unsatisfied, one seized the man and the other his mule.

"They believe him to be you, my lord," Veena murmured in concern.

"It appears so. They are evidently on the lookout for me, so anyone who bears any resemblance is subject to detention. That being the case, these rags are not likely to fool them. My height will give me away, and the same goes for you, Nai Lancaster," he said grimly.

The unfortunate prisoner was saved any further harassment when one of the guards whistled, and from a nearby roadside hut stepped a man familiar to them all.

Veena drew in her breath sharply. "Samrit Udom!" she gasped. "He knows us all too well to be fooled by any disguises. We can't go any farther."

It was maddening. Through the gate, across the moat, down a shaded road lined with the graceful spires of wats lay the river, flowing toward faraway Bangkok and safety. Freedom so near, yet so far. It was useless to try to force their way through. They had no weapons, and doubtless the hut held other guards with swords, itching to use them.

"We'd better retreat before that devil Udom casts a glance this way," David murmured. "We'll try the Suan Prung Gate leading southward. There may be no guard there, as it doesn't lead directly to the river, like this one."

"You are right. Come." Taksin hoisted Sawitri to his shoulder and began to force a way through the surging crowd.

It was hard going until they reached a rough track leading off from the road, southwest through trees and scrub. Now there were fewer people here and they were able to press on without hindrance.

With the south gate in sight, they paused to take stock. Here there were also two guards, but they lounged together on a wooden bench, making no attempt to halt any who passed by.

"With luck we might pass as coolies," Taksin murmured. "I could stoop to disguise my height."

"And I could feign lameness." David searched around among the bushes bordering the path until he found a length of stout bamboo. Using this as a walking stick, he leaned heavily on it, and dragged his left foot as he moved slowly forward, a perfect illustration of lameness.

The others fell in about him, and now they presented a picture of abject poverty with their rags and physical disabilities. There was nothing to distinguish them from other frightened citizens, escaping with what they could carry from the advancing marauders.

"Here comes a large family group. Let them pass us and keep just behind," Veena urged. "That way we'll be subjected to less scrutiny."

They followed her advice, pressing close behind the limping old grandfather with his numerous offspring about him, and so passing unchallenged through the gates and out to safety.

Once out of sight of the guards, they dropped their subterfuge and hurried on until they felt themselves at a safe distance. Then they paused to consider their next move.

"Somehow I must reach Bangkok and talk with the King," Taksin said. "I've no idea where his advancing army is, but once they reach Chiengmai, they'll get to grips with the Shans and, armed as they'll be, should drive them out eventually."

"I, too, shall make for the capital," David decided. "It will be best to leave Selina and the children there in safety while I return to see how the teak camps are faring, and if our bungalow is still standing for them to go back to."

Veena nodded her agreement. "And to reach it, with three young children, the Ping River is our only practical way."

"Decidedly. We must join it as soon as possible and try to buy a boat or hire passages. May Buddha be praised that I was not searched and my money confiscated," Taksin said.

David nodded.

"That goes for me, too. Even so, it could take a week or ten days to reach Bangkok, depending on the kind of boat."

They left the track, taking an even rougher one that led in the direction of the river. When they reached it, they found a considerable number of people, all looking anxiously for river transport, but finding nothing at all to be had at this tiny collection of shacks.

Out on the water it was a different story. Boats of various sizes were being paddled frantically downriver, all filled to capacity with people, bundles and even a few animals, fleeing from the threatened city.

"We seem to be too late already," Veena said in dismay.

"For the small craft," Taksin agreed. "Our only hope is to bribe a passage on a rice barge. Keep a sharp lookout for any sizable craft that isn't already packed."

One or two passed by in midstream. A few of the waiting refugees called out, begging passages, or offering small sums in return for transportation. These pleas were all ignored.

"They'll relent if the bribe is high enough," David said with cynicism. "Fortunately, we have the means to outbid most of these poor devils."

When the next rice barge approached, he called out boldly, offering a sum large enough to tempt most captains of these squat vessels plying to and fro with their burdens of grain.

The captain, in oil-stained shirt and battered straw hat, hesitated, then steered his boat toward a bamboo landing platform jutting out on piles.

"Not two families," he declared, eyeing the four adults and three children dispassionately. "I'm overloaded already. I'll take half of you if you pay in advance."

"You go," Taksin urged, turning to David. "You have two children to consider. I'll take my chance on the next one."

There was no alternative. David wished them good luck and lifted his two youngsters aboard. They all waved madly as the craft made her way back into midstream and sailed off toward Bangkok.

Sawitri seemed about to howl with mortification at being left behind. Veena diverted her by telling her to keep a sharp lookout for another rice barge when they, too, could be off.

It was some time before they spotted one. Taksin, growing uneasy in case any of the Shans, having found he had fled from his palace, should come this way looking for him, roared out to the man at the steering wheel. "Are you in charge? Take us aboard and drop us anywhere that suits you and you can name your own price."

"My own price, eh?" The dumpy barge was steered in their direction, to their intense relief.

"I'm bound for Bangkok," the captain told them, "but I've barely a square inch left aboard. Everybody wants to escape from the city."

If Taksin could only reveal his identity, this man would surely be glad to serve him, and forever afterward boast how he had saved the governor's life, Veena reflected. But such a course was impossible with so many listening ears.

"We ask nothing more than to get away from here," Taksin declared. "Perhaps we could transfer to some larger boat farther downstream if you can't take us all the way."

"You have a friendly, honest face, and a comely wife and child," the barge man said. "It would be a pity to leave you to the mercy of the Shans or the jungle creatures. There's only one place aboard I could accommodate you. My own sleeping cabin. It's only a cramped cupboard of a place, but you can have it if you wish for what money you can afford. I'll stretch out somewhere on deck."

"May Buddha reward you!" Taksin thrust Sawitri up toward the deck, then helped up Veena before the other clamoring refugees grew bolder and swamped the boat. He had barely time to scramble aboard himself before the barge pushed off again, and they were safely on their way.

The cabin to which they were ushered was just as its owner had described it. A dim little cupboard in the bows with a tiny porthole to give light and air. Shelves full of junk occupied one end, with a rickety table and chair in front. A bunk bed was stretched across the opposite side, just wide enough to take two at a pinch.

"The best I can do," the captain said. "Take it or leave it."

"I'm grateful to you." Taksin passed him a sum of money that brought profuse thanks.

"There'll be rice and vegetables cooked later on if you come up for it," he said as he went back to work.

"Thanks, but we have enough food for the present."

Veena eyed their refuge ruefully. "A far cry from the palace and your usual affluence, my lord," she sighed.

"I'll survive. At least it offers safety. The palace is almost certainly looted by now and maybe burned out. I have a strange feeling that I'll never reign there as governor again."

She stared in dismay. "But it is your whole life, lord. You had so many plans for improving the lot of the people. What will you do if you don't return when the Shans are driven back?"

"Who can say? I must talk with the King first. So much has happened lately, and the assassination of the princess and her father has changed the set plans. From my point of view it is a welcome release, but should I take up the reins later, it will all begin again. The pressure from the King to marry someone of whom he approves, the strain of living always in the public eye. In comparison, a coolie's life is easier."

She clearly understood. Fundamentally, he was as much a serf of the King as any poverty-stricken farmer, since the sovereign had the power to banish or even execute him for treason. As a distant member of the royal family he must bow to the royal decrees or stand in peril.

"Fate has dealt harshly with you, my lord," she murmured, thinking of the beautiful statue by the lake. "It is understandable that you rebel against it, yet you were born for high office and fill it superbly."

"I was also born for happiness, my sweet one. Happiness and love."

He grasped her hands. The cramped space seemed to shut out the world, enclosing them in a secret sanctuary where nothing else mattered except themselves. They were so close that she felt the warmth of his superb body, and the pulse beating madly for her. She saw the naked desire, agonizingly aware that her whole being answered his call with equal passion.

"My lord, the child," she murmured huskily.

He sighed deeply, and seemed to awake from a trance.

"We had better go up on deck for a while," he said. "The danger is past for the time being."

There was barely room to move, with people and bundles littering every vacant space. Presently the captain, conscious that this family had paid much more than any of the others, cleared a way to a squat bale of cotton, and this made a comfortable resting place from which to watch the passing scene.

When Sawitri became restless, Veena diverted her by singing little songs, or telling nursery stories. Taksin sat apparently deep in somber thought, surely preoccupied with the future and what it would hold for him. She herself was glad she could not give her mind to what lay ahead. It was enough for the moment that she sat with her lord as an equal, his body against hers, poignantly sweet.

They remained on deck until the sun sank low, refusing the food that the other refugees eagerly accepted, and quenching their thirst with sweet, juicy pomelos. Then, as the motley crowd prepared to stretch out head to toe for the night, they made for the privacy of their tiny cabin.

Here they enjoyed a meal from what they had brought with them, and by the time they had finished it was rapidly growing dark in the confined space. Sawitri, drooping with fatigue and the excitement of the day, was undressed and put to sleep on the bunk, and Veena was alone with her lord.

There was nowhere to sit except the one rickety chair.

"You must share the bunk with Sawitri, my lord," she said. "I can manage quite well on the floor when I'm tired of sitting on the chair."

"Oh no! For this brief passage we are equals, my sweet. I refuse to be set on a pedestal any longer. In spite of the menace that forced us to flee the city and the squalid conditions we now endure, I feel great happiness, because no barriers come between us. All the pomp is swept away, and we are like the poor coolie families around us, so no more deference, please."

Seizing her, he lifted her in his athletic arms and placed her on the bunk beside his sleeping child. His arms still around her, he stood looking down on her, his expression veiled by the deepening gloom.

Her face was like a pale lotus blossom beneath him. Her heart beat so fast that she was breathless and speechless in a great surge of emotion. He felt the tension and bent toward her until his dark head rested on her breasts. She shuddered with sensuous delight.

"I want you, my lotus blossom, here and now," he murmured hoarsely.

Jolted back to stark reality, she came to her senses. This was not the time or place to explore the heights and the depths of love as they had once done together. Then, the circumstances had been different. The enchanted hush of a ruined city about them, the knowledge of Taksin's imminent marriage that would set an unbridgeable barrier between them. Now there was only squalor and pressing anxiety as to his future, and hers, with the forlorn hope that perhaps by some miracle they could one day belong to each other in the eyes of the world, as well as each other.

"No, my lord," she breathed, with an effort that cost her dearly. "Now that you are free, we must wait and hope for the right moment. The bond between us is too precious to risk in furtive squalor. You are my revered lord and master, and I adore you. It will always be so. Naturally I pray that the time will come when we can marry and live in honorable harmony for the rest of our lives. Is that too much to ask?"

He sighed. "Not for you. I could never take you as a concubine. It must be all or nothing."

The darkness had stolen upon them unawares. They could barely see each other's faces. He bent and kissed her gently on the mouth, then curled up on the floor for the most uncomfortable night of his life.

CHAPTER FIFTEEN

It was strange and exciting to be in Bangkok, the great capital that hugged the Menam Chao Phraya and sprawled over onto the opposite bank in its twin city, Thonburi. The traffic of oxcarts, samlors, rickshaws and handcarts was denser, the noise more penetrating, the temples bigger, more ornate and more numerous. Veena loved the temples with their delicate, tinkling bells that sounded at the least vibration of the wind, like celestial bells rung by the gods.

The monsoon had now descended on the land. Dense rainstorms swept the city most afternoons, keeping Veena and Sawitri indoors, and after their passing the air was warm, close and heavy with humidity. The two were staying in a small private hostelry for women, while Taksin was at the palace conferring with the King.

Veena was consumed with anxiety on his behalf. They had been in the capital for several days now, and still he had not come to tell her the outcome of the talks. She felt certain that he would have spoken of his love for her and his desire to marry her, and feared the King's reaction.

It would have been some comfort if she could have been united with Selina and her children again, but she had no idea of where they were staying. The city had a considerable influx of refugees, waiting until the danger in the north was past and the invaders driven out, and Veena thought it wise to remain quietly incognito in her retreat on the outskirts until Taksin's position became clear.

She and Sawitri were sitting in a flower-covered pergola in the garden one afternoon when to her intense joy she saw Taksin striding toward them. Sawitri leaped to her feet and into his arms, to be hugged and kissed and presented with a bright new ball that he had bought for her on the way.

Off she ran around the garden paths, bouncing her new toy, and Taksin and Veena were free to talk.

"I've been quite anxious," she said. "You seemed to be so long away, my lord. Have the talks gone well?"

A shadow crossed his face. "No. He is furious with me for wanting to marry a commoner. He asks why I cannot take you as a concubine and marry someone more suitable that he will find for me. I told him I would never consent to that."

"So what will he do?" Her voice was controlled but her spirit plummeted.

"Unless I conform, he will banish me from the land, leaving everything I possess behind. It will be hard, starting again in a strange land without a baht, but easier by far than bowing to the yoke and being a gilded puppet with a wife I abhor and duties that would be intolerable under those circumstances. With you beside me, I can win through anywhere. Say you understand, my love."

"I would gladly follow you to the ends of the earth, my lord," she said passionately, "but how can I steal Sawitri's birthright and keep my self-esteem? She has already lost so much in the lake tragedy. How can I take away any more?"

He sighed. "I, too, hate the thought of depriving her, but wealth and position are not paramount in a child's life. Surely a happy and stable family atmosphere count for more."

True, but could there be happy stability for any of them, banished to a strange land, with different languages and customs, she reflected. No doubt the King would force him to relinquish even his name, for fear of bringing disgrace to his own illustrious family. Even the staunchest love might die under such circumstances. For herself, she could endure any hardship, but never could she inflict it on the two she loved best.

"When do you have to give him your answer?" she asked.

"Tomorrow. This night he has commanded me to spend in a

monastery, meditating and praying. He insists that it will give me the courage to return to Chiengmai and my duties there as soon as the city is free of the Shans. I shall bow to his wishes in passing a night of penance, but am sure it will make no difference to my feelings."

"Then we'll speak no more of the future until tomorrow, my lord," she said, in spite of the effort it cost her.

"As you wish. I shall come to you at dawn in the hope that our minds are as one."

He took his evening meal with them before going off to do penance. The good-night kiss had been sweet and poignant, more so on Veena's part because deep down in her heart she knew that it was farewell. At least for the time being.

Already her mind was made up that whatever it cost her, she must not be the cause of ruining Taksin's life and that of his child. It would be too great a burden for her to bear. He was not fashioned for menial, ill-paid work, which was all he was likely to get as an outcast in a strange land, but for wise and esteemed governorship and high life. With her disappearance, he would take up his rightful position again, and perhaps even find someone more fitting to love and comfort him.

That hurt. If she dithered all through the night she might weaken, so as soon as Sawitri was asleep, she hurried through the still-busy streets toward the great river, after leaving a note for Taksin.

Escape. She had thought it all out. She would make her way to the Lak Mo mission station, a Catholic foundation that rescued orphaned and abandoned girl babies, brought them up and taught them a trade such as silkworm rearing and silk weaving, so that they could earn a living later on. She had done part of her early training there, caring for the sick babies and teaching the older children what she could. Mother Maria, the nun in charge, was sweet and understanding. She would be glad to have her back for a time, and as the mission was situated in a small, out-of-the-way town, she would be safe from any remaining Shans or detection by Taksin.

He would be grief-stricken when he found only her note in the morning. The thought of it cut deep. How glad she was that she had ended it on a note of hope, a straw to save them both from drowning in sorrow.

"I promise to return to you in one year's time," she had written. "If at that time you are still in the same mind, and anxious to renounce everything for me, I shall capitulate. In the meantime, may the Lord Buddha watch over you and Sawitri, and keep you well and happy."

Having left everything except a change of clothes behind in their hurried flight from Chiengmai, she had little to carry with her. However, like Taksin, she had hidden what money she possessed on her person, so knew that hiring a boat passage would be no problem. The Lak Mo mission was situated on a klong leading off from the Chao Phraya River about fifty miles north of Bangkok. It was about halfway between the capital and Chiengmai, so she should reach it in a few days' time, if a passage could be had immediately.

She was glad to reach the comparative calm of the great river and leave the streets, daunting for a lone girl after dark, behind. In the moonlight, the water stretched black and sinister across to the far side, but along the near bank, crazy shanties of wood, bamboo and rice straw matting jostled each other in neighborly squalor. Washing festooned the entrances, fowls clucked sleepily from coops, dogs scavenged around, while the owners worked like a swarm of ants on various tasks, helped by the light of hanging lanterns.

There were no rice barges to be seen here, only family boats used for fishing, getting around and transporting commodities to local markets. Veena made her way along the crowded bank until she reached a rather larger boat. The owners were busy loading the squat, wide, bargelike vessel with produce. Pomelos, papayas, mangos, durians, pineapples and many more local fruits were being piled around the center structure, which was nothing more than a flimsy awning to give shade from the fiercest heat of the day.

The family looked friendly, Veena decided. Father, mother and two teenaged daughters, loading up ready to be off to some upriver market at first light of dawn. With competition so keen, an early start was essential if they wished to sell their fruit before rivals beat them to it.

This vessel could not take her far, she realized, but far enough to transfer to some more powerful boat. If she lingered here waiting for better transport, Taksin would surely come searching for her after he had read the note. So without further hesitation, she called to the woman, asking when they were sailing and if she could go with them.

"At dawn," the woman answered, "but only a short distance up to the morning market. You are welcome to come if you wish."

Veena told her that she was a refugee from the trouble in the north, adding that she had friends in Lak Mo if she could reach them. This touched the heart of the mother, who invited her to spend the night with them, sleeping alongside her daughters, so that she would be ready at dawn to sail with them.

Veena gratefully accepted, shared their late meal and slept soundly for the next few hours.

It was scarcely light, with a dense mist over the river, when they set off, the father and mother sitting one on either side of the boat, propelling themselves along with their great poles. Soon the mist began to rise in gray swirls, the sun broke through and the passing scene took on a magical beauty.

Instead of the squalid shanties that hugged the banks near the capital, there was only the wide shining water lined by jungle. Palm trees stretched their huge leaves out over the river, mingling with tree ferns and plantains, the whole covered with creepers and vines, to form a dense green barrier. It was unbelievably lovely, and in spite of her sorrow at having cut herself off from Taksin, she felt a welcome peace steal over her as she exchanged places with the mother to take her turn with the pole.

They reached the market town. The river here was already congested with the boats of other vendors selling almost everything, but they found a mooring place and Veena disembarked. The kindly couple waved aside her offered payment, so with many thanks she left them and made her way toward a substantial jetty, where larger craft, plying their trade up and down the river, put in to buy food and other commodities.

The sight of a portable refreshment stall wedged between fish and vegetable stalls reminded her that she was both thirsty and hungry. The stall was nothing more than two large flat baskets set down on the ground, connected by a yoke, which the owner shouldered when she wanted to move on. One basket held pots of rice, beans and curries, while the other held small urns of tea and coffee kept warm by a tiny stove. Veena bought a glass of tea, and rice served on a piece of palm leaf, then, refreshed, turned her steps toward the jetty.

She was pleased to see a teakwood rice barge tied up, which had evidently lain overnight, for the owner was preparing to depart.

"Up- or downriver?" she called.

"Up."

"Can you take me to where the klong diverges for the Lak Mo mission station?"

He nodded, naming the modest sum.

She boarded, paid the passage money and was given a space in the covered part of the barge, curtained off from the rest.

Conditions on this short trip would be much better than when fleeing from Chiengmai, she reflected. Instead of being crowded with refugees, the boat carried only its cargo of rice, together with the owner, his wife and son.

They left soon after, and now the going was almost luxurious. Veena sat happily astern in a rickety deck chair shaded by a plate-like straw hat, watching the passing river traffic and the changing scenes on the banks. At midday, a sudden downpour drove her under cover, to join the family in their meal, after which she took a rest in her own niche.

The sky had cleared and the sun was shining again when she later emerged on deck, to resume her seat in the stern until approaching night signaled time for the evening meal.

So passed the next three days until arrival at the small town where a peaceful klong diverged for Lak Mo. Here Veena disembarked and hired another small boat to transport her to the village, about five miles away.

It was reached at midday, and a short distance farther on, set peacefully in a jungle clearing, the mission station came into view.

With a rush of nostalgia, she left the river and entered the enclosed compound, neatly kept by the nuns and older pupils, and bright with flowering shrubs. Frangipani scented the air, and flambuoyants made great splashes of scarlet by the bamboo fencing.

In the center of this stood the mission station, a plain utility structure set high on stilts, with wooden steps leading up to the platform-verandah surrounding it. Teak panels formed the walls, and the bamboo and thatched roof overhung deeply to give protection from sun and rain. The windows were small openings covered only by mosquito netting and the entrance was softened by a creeping, pink-flowered vine.

Refreshingly uncluttered after the crowded shanties clinging like barnacles to the river's edge, Veena reflected as she mounted the steps and walked into the little reception office.

The nun seated at the desk stared for a moment then recognized her as one of their former assistants.

"Veena, how nice to see you again," she said, rising. "What brings you here and how long are you staying?"

"Quite a while, if you'll have me. I'm in need of a peaceful retreat after the last weeks," Veena said.

Sister Claire nodded. "The Shan rebellion, you mean? It must have been hard for you. Father Joseph is here with us and often wondered what had become of you after the governor and his staff fled. He'll be very glad to see you and you'll have a lot to tell each other I'm sure. You'll find him in our little hospital, no doubt."

It was out in the back compound, built in the same fashion as the main building, but much smaller. Veena went across, smiling at the small girls playing nearby, and entered the building where she had worked several years back.

Father Joseph was in the records office, writing notes on case sheets. He wrung her hands warmly, pressed her into a bamboo chair and poured out a cool drink.

"Now tell me how you escaped, my child."

"First you tell me how you got away and what is happening in Chiengmai and especially to the clinic, Father."

He smiled. "Happily, we heard only this morning that the soldiers sent from Bangkok have succeeded in restoring order and driving out the Shans. Those not killed or captured have retreated back to the border hills. Some damage has been inflicted on the city, especially the governor's palace, but nothing that cannot be rectified. Fortunately, they left my mission standing intact after looting it of drugs. They were after more valuable loot than I possessed."

"Well, I'm glad you thought of this refuge and got away in time or they might have killed you. When are you thinking of going back and restoring order to your little world?"

"I mean to start off tomorrow. Why don't you come with me, as you seem to have left your young charge. Your help would be appreciated."

She shook her head. "Later perhaps, but not yet, Father. I'm in need of a quiet retreat and this is perfect." She went on to tell him of her hurried departure from the palace, along with the governor and David Lancaster and family, then, knowing she could trust him completely, confided her private problem and her solution to it.

He nodded understandingly. "I think you are right to give him a cooling off period, and yourself too. It would have been a drastic step for him to take, to throw over everything and flout the King. Now he'll have the chance to get everything in perspective, and you too."

"I suppose you've heard nothing of David and family?" she asked, to change the harrowing subject.

"Nothing, but I expect he'll drift back to Chiengmai like all the others now. Do you mean to let him know where you are?"

"I think not for the moment. You may tell him I'm safe and well and will get in touch later."

So Veena settled into an ordered routine in this peaceful sanctuary, helping out in the hospital and wherever else she was needed. Off-duty it was a delight to wander through the well-kept compounds and cultivated grounds, where planning and hard work provided most of what the mission needed, making it almost self-supporting. Small banana and papaya groves sheltered beds of pineapples, watermelons and vegetables. Piglets, chickens and ducks rooted and scratched around in their own stout pens. Goats provided milk, and a couple of oxen brute force for the heavier work.

But the section Veena liked most was that devoted to the rearing of silkworms. Mulberry shrubs made a pleasant green patch on which the grubs fed, after which they were nursed through the chrysalis stage, and then the silk thread unwound from the fat yellow cocoons to be processed by some of the older pupils. Timing at this stage was vital, before the Bombycidae moths gnawed their way out, so ruining the long strands. The finished silk was lustrous, strong and beautiful, and commanded a good price when sold to city merchants to help finance the mission.

She had been there about a month and settled into an ordered, not unpleasant routine, where only the nights brought sadness. Waking often to the weird and varied jungle calls pressing in on the mission, the thought of Taksin would come crowding in on her to fill her entire being with aching longing. Was he back in Chiengmai, and was he chafing at the circumstances that had driven them apart, as she was?

One morning at breakfast the sister in charge set her heart beating faster when she mentioned from the head of the table that Father Joseph would be paying them a visit today.

"He's bringing out some drugs and medical supplies that were running low," she added. "You might make up the spare room bed for him, Veena, since he will be staying overnight."

Now, Veena thought feverishly, she would find out exactly what was happening in Chiengmai, and whether Taksin had returned to his palace to supervise its restoration.

It was an effort to keep her mind on teaching a class of small girls plain sewing. She was glad when she could dismiss them and stroll out to the klong to watch out for the welcome boat.

It arrived at last. Father Joseph stepped ashore, set the boat boy to carry up the supplies, then greeted her warmly yet with an expression of unease that instantly communicated itself to her. Suddenly she was afraid to ask about Taksin.

"How are things in the city? Have David and his family returned to their bungalow?" she asked jerkily.

He nodded. "Fortunately, it was untouched, so they came back days ago. They were all concerned for you and demanding to know where you were, but I kept it secret as you wished."

"Thank you. I'll get in touch as soon as I can." She tried to voice her greatest concern, but the words stuck in her throat.

"Chiengmai is recovering quickly," he went on. "Fortunately, the damage was not extensive. Even the palace is getting back to normal."

"And Taksin in occupation?" There, it was out with a rush.

"I'm afraid not. Another governor has been appointed. A young married man with two sons."

"Another governor?" Dismay and apprehension mingled in her tone. "Then where is he?"

Father Joseph took both her hands in a gesture of compassion. "This is going to come as a shock, my dear. The rumor goes that he is dead. The citizens believe he was killed while trying to escape from the Shans, but you and David know different. David is forced to hold his tongue on pain of instant dismissal from his post and deportation from Siam."

Veena went white to the lips. Father Joseph placed a comforting arm around her and drew her toward the mission.

"Come and sit down, my dear. You look absolutely bowled over. And don't take it too much to heart, as there's no proof of anything."

Feeling like death herself, she stumbled up to the mission with the help of his sustaining arm. True, Taksin had not been killed in the escape, but what had become of him? Had the King already banished him from his native land, never to be seen there again? Worse still, was he really dead, as the rumors went, executed for treason and disobeying the King's command?

CHAPTER SIXTEEN

The rainy season, with all its attendant humidity and discomfort, was at an end. Now the best season of all lay ahead. Clear warm days and cooler nights that could be enjoyed to the full. Ploughing and rice planting would go ahead, along with other farming activity. The rivers and klongs were full, the land would bloom, festivals would take place and life would be a little less irksome for all who toiled for their living.

Life at the mission reflected the change. The sisters and older pupils spent all their spare time in the vegetable plots, singing their harmonious Christian hymns and laughing with sheer happiness. Their god whom they called Jesus encouraged them to believe that life was meant to be enjoyed, at variance with Lord Buddha who taught that humility and affliction were necessary states to be endured with good grace as a step to a better life in the next reincarnation.

If so, she herself was paying heavily at the moment for future serenity. She had still heard nothing of Taksin, and the heart had gone from her life. She performed her tasks like a puppet and the future stretched gray and bleak ahead.

Until one fabulous morning when the sister in charge drew her aside. "I have heard from Father Joseph, my dear. He says I am to tell you that he is on his way here with someone special. He should be here tomorrow."

The blood rushed to Veena's cheeks. In her low state she felt giddy and weak with a blinding flash of hope. Could it possibly be *him?*

Sister Claire, not being in Veena's confidence regarding Taksin, could only speculate, but was pleased at the hope of any development that could lift Veena's spirits. She had been truly concerned for her these past weeks.

"Well, whoever it is, I hope something good comes of it," she added. "Your skills are not being utilized to the full out in this backwater. You are worthy of better things."

The rest of the day passed in a dream for Veena. She scarcely dare hope, yet the feverish anticipation would not be banished.

After a restless night, she gave up any pretense of working and made for the landing stage by the river. Here she mooned away the time until at last the expected boat came into view.

Was he there? She stared intently at the three figures. There were Father Joseph, the boat boy and Taksin. He was dressed not in the splendid attire he had worn when governor but as soberly as a coolie, with flat straw hat and dark glasses obscuring his handsome face, yet to her loving eyes he was unmistakable.

The boat drew level. He leaped out, careless of his safety, and gathered her in a swift embrace.

No words were adequate and none spoken. They simply stood locked together as time stood still and all the world was forgotten. When at length Veena surfaced, it was to see Father Joseph standing regarding them with kindly tolerance.

"Take your time," he said gently. "I'm sure you have much to talk about and not for other ears. I suggest you take a stroll by the river. I'll explain to Sister Claire that you will be in soon."

With a grateful smile in his direction, Veena took Taksin's hand and drew him away down the rough track. Few people ever went this way, so here was the blessed privacy they craved.

"I suppose Father Joseph told you where I was, my lord," she said. "I asked him to keep it secret from everyone for the time being, but after rumors of your death reached me I felt so wretched that I longed for news of you. How did the report come about?"

"That was the King's doing. He said if I would not conform to his wishes I would be obliterated from the family. I was kept under close arrest and a new governor appointed after the announcement of my fictitious death. I was not allowed to communicate with anyone, of course. That's why I couldn't set about finding you immediately when you ran away."

"But why change now? If you returned to Chiengmai, or anyone happened to recognize you, surely a crisis would arise."

"Without doubt. That is why I am here incognito, my love. You must never again refer to me as 'my lord.' I am plain Taksin Krong now to the end of my days. I am on oath not to go near Chiengmai or anywhere else where I might be recognized. I met Father Joseph at the junction of this klong and the river, and must return immediately the same way. I came only to collect you, if you will come with me as the wife of an ordinary man, shorn of the glamor he once knew."

Radiance suffused her face. "If I will come? I could ask nothing more of life! But I don't understand the King's magnanimity. Why is he being so indulgent to us both?"

"Chiefly because together we can be more use to him than if I'd been banished abroad. Also he was grateful to me for saving the palace treasures from being looted by hiding them in the cellars. But there are conditions, my love."

"Such as?"

"You may know of Phuket Island. It lies in the far south in the Andaman Sea. Few Siamese venture there. Although it belongs to Siam, the people are more Malay in outlook. It is a beautiful island with one great asset. Tin mining. This brings welcome revenue to the nation, but with development could bring much more. The manager there has recently been exposed as a rogue, lining his own pockets and neglecting the interests of the mines and workers. The king needs a trustworthy representative there as administrator of mines and island life. He has offered me the post, providing I keep up the identity of Taksin Krong and forget the past."

"But you can't know anything of tin mining."

"I can learn. Besides, the position will be purely administrative, to safeguard the interests of the nation. A new manager who knows the workings and techniques will be appointed to assist me."

"And where do I come in, I wonder?"

"In a position just made for you, my love. As matron of the hospital. It, too, has become rundown for lack of competent administration. You would only be there during the daytime. Evenings and nights would be our own. There is an attractive house where we would live right by the sea. Sawitri would be in her element."

"And so should I. Oh, Taksin, it all sounds too good to be true."

He nodded. "Better than being exiled to a foreign land, at least. Then it is settled?"

"Sealed with a kiss."

The lingering embrace was sweet beyond measure, and then, his lips against hers, he said, "We must catch Father Joseph before he leaves. There's an important ceremony to be performed. We spoke of it on the way here. He will be happy to marry us, my love."

"In spite of his different faith?"

"He says all sincere religion has something in common. It is the striving to live a good and worthwhile life and help one's fellow creatures that matters. He certainly lives up to his principles."

"That's true, and it gives him the same peace and satisfaction as depicted on the face of Lord Buddha," she agreed. "Now tell me, where is Sawitri all this while? She must have been so lonely, with you imprisoned and me far away."

"Oddly enough, she's quite happy in a private kindergarten in Bangkok, with other small children to play with and experienced people to look after her. Fortunately, that money I brought with me was never taken from me, so I'm well able to pay the fees. It will be nice to have her for the long vacations and she'll love running wild on Phuket."

Veena sighed with pure happiness. It was frightening for life to change so suddenly from black despair to radiant hope.

The ceremony in the sister's office, scented with frangipani, was simple and short. It was good to have Father Joseph's blessing, and to know that they belonged to each other, now and forever.

Afterward all three walked down to the boat together and were punted down the klong to where the larger boat, which had brought Taksin from Bangkok, waited on the river.

"A private boat belonging to the King," he explained to Veena. "It brought me here in secrecy and will take us back the same way."

They waved farewell to Father Joseph as he started back upstream for Chiengmai, while they were transported swiftly down the broad river toward the capital.

"This is a strange honeymoon, but sweeter than any fabulous aftermath of a sumptuous ceremony such as would have been my lot had not the Shans rebelled, wiping out the plans made for me," he said as they lay together in their small cabin that night. "Wicked though it sounds, I can't help but be glad of their intervention."

"I, too," confessed Veena. Without a penny or even a change of clothes, bound for an unknown island and life among strangers, she was still happier than she had ever been before. Together they could surely surmount every obstacle.

"What happens when we reach Bangkok?" she said presently. "Shall I have any opportunity to acquire any clothes, I wonder?"

"Neither of us will be allowed to land in Bangkok," he said. "I've given my word. The boat will only lie there for one night, so that the captain can renew supplies of food and fuel. But he is a reasonable man with a friendly wife. If I give them money, they'll buy a few things for us while they make their own purchases, so that we need not land on Phuket looking like a pair of rundown coolies."

She laughed. "I can see my new husband is a man of resource. I shall never need to worry with him at the helm."

The strange, idyllic voyage passed like a tranquil dream. In Bangkok they moored in a quiet backwater within sight of Wat Arun, the Temple of the Dawn. Gazing at it, Veena thought of the marriage ceremony she might have had there as an unimportant Siamese girl.

It would have been quite simple. Dressed in white, she and her partner would have knelt together, a single white cord wrapped round their heads joining them in a visible bond. Guests would

pour scented water over their heads, while in the background a
Buddhist monk might recite texts to bring blessings to the couple.

Not really a religious ceremony, so she did not feel deprived.
The brief service Father Joseph had performed for them had appeared more sacred and binding.

The captain and his wife brought several cotton blouses and
pasins, together with underwear and toilet articles for Veena, and
a serviceable outfit for Taksin.

"We can buy clothes more to our fancy later on Phuket," Taksin said. "It's not quite uncivilized, you know."

From Bangkok they sailed to the mouth of the Chao Phraya
and into the Gulf of Thailand. Now they were out in the open sea,
with a gentle breeze cooling the air and making life on deck pleasant.

"We shall reach Songkla tomorrow," the captain told them a
few days later. "That is as far as I go. There you must take a local
river boat across the Malay peninsula and so to Phuket Island."

It mattered little. They were in a dream world with no intru-
sions, and were in no hurry to surface.

Songkla was a large fishing port, so they had no difficulty in
hiring a passage on a vessel taking goods to Phuket. But in con-
trast to their idyllic voyage from the north, this boat was crowded
with passengers and merchandise, and there was no privacy left as
they sailed along the klong.

So they were glad when at last they landed on the island which
was to be their new home.

It was dusk, yet an air of festivity filled the air. People in their
best clothes thronged the street of the fishing village, while the
klong seemed to be alive with lights.

"Why of course, this is November! I'd forgotten in the press of
events," Veena said laughing. "We've arrived on my favorite festi-
val day, Coy Krathong. We can pretend that it is laid on just for
our benefit, to welcome us here."

Smiling, Taksin pulled out a coin and bought one of the tiny
boats from a street vendor. It was fashioned from a banana leaf,
and capable of floating for some time. Inside was a candle fixed
upright and a stick of incense. The vendor lit the candle, and

Veena launched it on the klong, along with the others, to give thanks to the water spirits for sending the rains.

How pretty they looked, like fairy boats in the deepening gloom, floating down an enchanted river.

"You need flowers, my love," he said, taking one of the frangipani wreaths that a vendor thrust upon him and fixing it on her hair. "Now you look like a true bride."

The scent was exquisite. It stole out from the grounds of a nearby temple and filled the air, while the night breeze from the sea rippled through the temple bells, setting them shivering with strange wild music.

"Now our union is complete," she murmured, "with the blessing of two great faiths. Our life will be happy here, my lord. Do not frown. That is the last time I shall call you 'my lord,' but in my heart you will always be just that. The one man in the world for me."

The lights on the klong floated away, growing dimmer and dimmer until they were gone, when Veena and Taksin turned away to find the dwelling that together they could make into a home.